D1091045

Raggedy Ann and Andy
The Second Treasury

RAGGEDY ANN AND ANDY
The Second Treasury

By Johnny Gruelle

Illustrated by the author
and by Worth Gruelle

LEMON TREE PRESS · NEW YORK

Originally published in three volumes as:

RAGGEDY ANN'S MAGICAL WISHES, Copyright © 1928 by Johnny Gruelle, Norwalk, Conn. Copyright renewed 1956 by Myrtle Gruelle.

RAGGEDY ANN IN THE MAGIC BOOK, Copyright © 1939 by Johnny Gruelle Company. Copyright Great Britain, 1939.

RAGGEDY ANN AND THE GOLDEN BUTTERFLY, Copyright © 1940 by Johnny Gruelle Company. Copyright Great Britain, 1940.

A Lemon Tree Press Book
Published in the United States of America in 1982 by
Galahad Books
95 Madison Avenue
New York, N.Y. 10016

Published by arrangement with The Bobbs-Merrill Company, Inc.

Library of Congress Catalog Card Number 82-82744

ISBN 0-88365-662-0

PRINTED IN THE UNITED STATES OF AMERICA

CONTENTS

Raggedy Ann's Magical Wishes

TO TWO LITTLE PLAYMATES

TEDDY G— and DICKIE G—

Raggedy Ann's Magical Wishes

By JOHNNY GRUELLE

Illustrated by the author

CHAPTER ONE

Little Neepy

ONE day when the real for sure folks had gone away from home and Raggedy Ann and Raggedy Andy had been left out in the little play-house in the orchard, Raggedy Ann said to Raggedy Andy, "Raggedy Andy, do you know what?"

"No, what?" Raggedy Andy asked in reply.

"Well sir!" Raggedy Ann smiled, "My magical Wishing Pebble which I have safe and sound, sewed up inside my cotton-stuffed body, is jiggling around!"

Raggedy Andy got to his wabbly cloth feet and stumped over to Raggedy Ann. "Let me see, Raggedy Ann!" he said, as he felt of Raggedy Ann's cotton-stuffed body with his rag hands. "Yes sir!" he laughed, "I can feel it jiggling around, Raggedy Ann. What do you s'pose can be the trouble with it?"

"Maybe it wants me to make a wish!" Raggedy Ann said; "I haven't made a wish for the longest, longest time, you know."

"I know it, Raggedy Ann!" Raggedy Andy said. "It seems ages and ages since we have had a lovely adventure! Do you s'pect we could have one today?"

"I s'pect we could, Raggedy Andy!" Raggedy Ann replied. "Marcella has forgotten she put us out here in the play-house and I am sure all the folks, even Dinah, the cook, have gone away!"

JOHNNY GRUELLE

"Why not make a wish to know when they will return?" Raggedy Andy asked. "Then," he continued, "we would know just how long we could have to hunt for an adventure!"

"That is a good idea, Raggedy Andy!" Raggedy Ann laughed. "Now remain real quiet and we shall soon see if the Wishing Pebble is as good as it used to be, or whether it has lost its magical power!"

Raggedy Andy remained real quiet, though he was very anxious.

He sat down beside Raggedy Ann.

Raggedy Ann smoothed out the wrinkles in her pretty white apron and covered both shoe-button eyes with her rag hands. Not that she had to do this when she made a wish with the magical Wishing Pebble. Oh, no! But Raggedy Ann covered her shoe-button eyes with her hands so that if there was any magic to be seen, she would see it in this manner.

"Aha! Raggedy Andy!" Raggedy Ann finally said, as she took her hands from her shoe-button eyes, "when I wished to know how long the folks would be away from home, I saw, just as if it were written in golden letters on a piece of paper, the words, 'Long enough.' So I s'pect we can start right out and hunt an adventure!"

Raggedy Andy hopped to his feet and ran to the little window in the play-house. He looked across the orchard towards the deep, deep woods. Then he ran to the door and looked out in that direction.

There was no one in sight. Old Bossy, the cow, was standing, sleepy-eyed, over in one corner of the fence, but cows did not count.

Since it was broad daylight, with the sun shining brightly, the Raggedys wanted to be certain that no real for sure person was about to watch them leave. "I can not see anyone, either coming down the road, or crossing the fields—or anywhere!" Raggedy Andy said, as he helped Raggedy Ann to her feet. Raggedy Andy always believed in being polite, and, as you very well know, it is always polite for a boy to help a girl in every possible way.

The Raggedys, catching hold of hands, raced across the orchard towards the fence. Old Bossy opened her eyes in amazement to see the Raggedy dolls running as they did, but Bossy did not say anything.

When they reached the fence, Raggedy Andy boosted Raggedy Ann through, for it was an old-fashioned rail fence; then he climbed through himself.

They scampered through some ferns and in a short time came to a lovely smooth path.

"I wish we had roller skates or something, so that we could just go scooting along the smooth path!" Raggedy Andy said.

"Wait a moment!" Raggedy Ann cried as she came to a stop. "Let's wish for something, Raggedy Andy! What do you say if I make a wish for two magical bicycles? The kind that will run by themselves without working our feet!"

"Ooh! That would be lovely, Raggedy Ann!" Raggedy Andy clapped his hands together and danced up and down at the thought.

"And all we shall have to do will be to jump on the bicycles and wish them to go and they will run by themselves! Oh! I think I shall wish for them right away, Raggedy Andy!"

"Please do, Raggedy Ann!" Raggedy Andy cried.

So Raggedy Ann made the wish, and before you could say Higledy Pigledy backwards, there stood two beautiful, shiny red bicycles with nickel plated handle bars and pedals and rubber tires and shiny bells and everything.

"How lovely!" Raggedy Andy cried, his little shoe-button eyes dancing with excitement.

"And thanks so much for making my wish come true, nice magical Wishing Pebble!" Raggedy Ann said as she patted the spot in her rag body where the Pebble was sewn!

Raggedy Andy helped Raggedy Ann upon her bicycle,

then he climbed upon his own and as soon as the Raggedys put their feet upon the pedals, the wonderful bicycles began to move.

As they went along, ringing the little bells and laughing and chatting about such wonderful magical things, they found that they could make the bicycles go as fast or as slow as they wanted, by just wishing, "Go faster!" or "Go slower!"

It was lovely riding this way through the wonderful, mysterious woods and as they turned a bend in the path, they came to a tiny house, not a bit larger than a dog-house and it was almost hidden beneath large ferns.

"I wonder who lives in such a cunning little house?" Raggedy Ann mused out loud as she brought her bicycle to a stop in front of the door.

"We shall soon see!" Raggedy Andy laughingly replied, knocking upon the door with his soft rag hand.

"Come in!" a little old man said as he held the little door open.

The Raggedys walked into the little house. "Why! Are you just moving in, or are you just moving out? There are no chairs to sit in!" Raggedy Andy said.

The little man looked very sad as he answered, "No! I am not just moving in, for I have lived here all the time, but I can't find a single chair growing in the woods on bushes, nor can I plant any chair seeds in that tin can and get the seeds to grow into chair bushes! So I just have to sit upon the hard, hard floor all the time!"

"We have never heard of chairs growing upon bushes!" Raggedy Ann said, "but we have known of nice dresses and clothes and shoes and slippers growing upon MAGICAL bushes, because we wished for them ourselves."

"I do not care for new clothes," the little man said, "but it would be nice to have chairs so that my friends could sit on them when they visit me!"

Raggedy Andy whispered to Raggedy Ann, "Don't you remember, Raggedy Ann, you have a magic Wishing Pebble sewed up inside your cotton-stuffed body?"

"Why! I had forgotten all about it, Raggedy Andy!" Raggedy Ann replied. "I shall wish for a lot of nice little chairs for the little man!" And as soon as she wished for them, there stood the little chairs. The little man was so pleased he went out in his little garden and picked sixteen red lolly-pops for the Raggedys to eat as they visited. Then Raggedy Ann wished for some jelly cake and ice-cream and chocolate candy and butter-scotch and they sat in the little chairs and rocked as they enjoyed the goodies.

Neepy—that was the little man's name—was very glad the Raggedys had come to see him. As they sat and talked with Neepy, there came a loud thump upon Neepy's little front door.

The thump was so loud, Neepy jumped right out of his chair.

"I smell goodies!" a gruff voice outside said. "Open the door so that I can come in and have some!"

"Dear me!" Raggedy Ann said, "Who can that rude person be, Neepy?"

Before Neepy could reply, there was a
and a push and the little door flew open
Gruffy Bear. "I smell goodies!" he said as
the crumbs of the jelly cake and at the emp
which the Raggedys and Neepy had had ice-cre

"Why, Mister Gruffy Bear," Neepy said, "we h
finished eating all the goodies and there isn't anything ...!"

"I'll just snoop in the cupboard and see!" Gruffy Bear said. "I'm sure you have some more jelly cake hidden!" And Gruffy Bear snooped in Neepy's cupboard.

"I can't find even a smidgin!" Gruffy Bear howled, "and the more I snoop around the hungrier I get for jelly cake! If you do not tell me where you have hidden it, I shall huff and puff and blow the roof right off this little house! That's what I shall do!"

"Honest, Mister Gruffy Bear," Neepy said, "all the jelly cake and the ice-cream and the chocolate candy and the butter-scotch have been eaten up!"

"What?" Gruffy Bear howled, "You had ice-cream and chocolate candy and butter-scotch, the nice things I like, and you didn't save me any?"

"I am sorry, Mister Gruffy Bear," little Neepy said, "but how were we to know that you were coming? We just ate everything because everything was so good."

"That is just what makes me so angry!" Gruffy Bear howled. "So now I guess maybe I'd better eat you up first, then I'll eat your two friends up next!" And he pointed to Raggedy Ann and Raggedy Andy.

"No sir!" Raggedy Ann said. "You shan't eat anyone up!"

"Yes, I shall!" Gruffy Bear shouted. "I shall eat Mister Neepy first! Do you want me to start at your feet, or at the top of your head?" he asked little Neepy.

"I tell you where you can start!" Raggedy Andy said, as he gave Gruffy Bear a push which sent him rolling out of Neepy's little house, "you can start eating grass, or s, for you shan't even nibble little Neepy!" Then Raggedy Andy slammed the door shut and locked it before old Gruffy Bear could get upon his feet. "Now!" said Raggedy Andy, "let's have some more goodies just for fun and we will teach Gruffy a lesson for being so rude!" And so they all had lots more ice-cream and cake and other nice things.

"Oooh!" Gruffy Bear cried when he got to his feet and came back to the door, "I smell goodies plainer than I did before! I must have some! Open the door or I shall open it myself!"

"I have locked the door, old Mister Gruffy Bear!" Raggedy Andy said, "and now we are having ice-cream and cake all over again to teach you not to be so rude! People who ask for things nicely always receive them, but people who are rude and ill-mannered never get nice things!"

Gruffy Bear sniffed at the crack in the door, "Oooh!" he said, "I can smell the jelly cake as plain as anything! You'd better hurry and open the door before I huff and puff and blow the door in!"

"Maybe we had better open the door before he really huffs and puffs and blows it in!" little Neepy said as he looked from Ann to Andy.

"No sir!" Raggedy Andy laughed. "Do not let old Mister Gruffy Bear fool you that way, Mister Neepy! Gruffy Bear has read a story about the three little pigs and he can't huff and puff the door in at all!"

"If you don't hurry and unlock the door, I'll show you!" Gruffy Bear howled. "I can smell the jelly cake and ice-cream so plain it makes me want it more than ever! I'll count three and then I'll start and huff and puff!"

"Don't pay any attention to him!" Raggedy Ann told little Neepy, "and he will get tired and go away after awhile!"

"Now I shall start!" Gruffy Bear howled, "ONE, TWO, THREE!" and he huffed as loud as he could, then he puffed as loud as he could.

"He makes the door rattle!" little Neepy said. "Shall I open it?"

Mercy! how Gruffy Bear huffed and puffed! He really could huff and puff a lot louder than the wolf huffed and puffed in The-Three-Little-Pigs story and the door rattled and shook. Then Gruffy Bear, seeing that he could not huff and puff the door in, got back and jumped with all his might at the door, and with a loud crash, the door came down and Gruffy Bear rolled into Neepy's little house. "Now give me the jelly cake and the ice-cream, or I shall eat all of you up!" he cried as he got upon his feet.

But the Raggedys only laughed, because there wasn't any cake left except a few little crumbs and there wasn't any ice-cream at all. "Ha!" Gruffy Bear cried, "I shall eat you up first!" And he caught Raggedy Andy. But Raggedy Andy wasn't so easily fooled as Gruffy Bear thought, for as soon as Gruffy caught Andy, Andy caught Gruffy and they wrestled and wrestled until Raggedy Andy wrestled old Mister Gruffy Bear right out of the house and pushed him "Splash!" right in the brook. "Whee!" little Neepy and Raggedy Ann cried. "Raggedy Andy was the best wrestler! So now we will have some cream puffs!"

So Raggedy Ann wished for some cream puffs and they sat upon the grass to eat them.

Old Mister Gruffy Bear was all wet and soppy when he climbed out of the brook and he came over near the Raggedys and little Neepy and shook himself.

"Here!" Raggedy Ann cried, "don't shake yourself around here! You shake water all over us!"

"That's just what I wanted to do!" Gruffy Bear said. "I see you are eating cream puffs and I want some!"

"I should think when Raggedy Andy wrestled you into the brook that it would teach you not to bother us any more!" Raggedy Ann said.

"Ha, ha, ha!" Old Mister Gruffy Bear laughed. "The only reason Raggedy Andy could wrestle me was because I let him! that's what!"

"Of course, you let him!" Raggedy Ann replied; "Because why? Because you could not help letting him! Raggedy Andy is a lot better wrestler than you are!"

"Don't you believe it!" Old Mister Gruffy Bear said. "I was all tired from huffing and puffing at Mister Neepy's door! And as soon as I get rested and eat six, or seven of your cream puffs, then we will wrestle again and I will throw Raggedy Andy in the brook! Then I will throw little Neepy into the brook, then I will throw Raggedy Ann into the brook, then I will throw Neepy's little house into the brook and then I will throw—no!" Gruffy Bear corrected himself, "I won't throw anything else in the brook! Just all of you and the house! Now give me the cream puffs! Every one of them!"

"You shan't have a single one, Mister Gruffy Bear!" Raggedy Ann said, "not until you learn how to ask for them, nice and polite!"

"Then I will take them away from you!" shouted Gruffy Bear, as he started to grab the cream puffs from Raggedy Ann.

"Wait a minute!" Raggedy Andy said.

"Why should I wait?" Gruffy Bear howled. "Can't you

see I am getting hungrier and hungrier and hungrier every minute? And the hungrier I get, the angrier I get and in a few minutes I shall get so angry, I am afraid I shall eat you all up!"

"We will have to wrestle again, I guess!" Raggedy Andy said, as he rolled up his sleeves. "And I guess I will have to wrestle you in the brook again!"

"I don't want to wrestle again!" Old Mister Gruffy Bear shouted. "I told you that I was getting angrier and angrier! You don't want me to eat you up, do you?" But Raggedy Andy didn't answer Gruffy Bear again; instead, Raggedy Andy wrestled Gruffy Bear right down to the brook and pushed him in again.

"Now let's run and hide from him, so he can't find us!" Raggedy Ann suggested.

JOHNNY
GRUELLE

CHAPTER TWO

Gruffy Bear

SO while Old Mister Gruffy Bear was climbing up the bank, his clothes all wet and soppy, the Raggedys and little Neepy ran through the woods and hunted for a nice place to hide.

"Oh! I just thought of a place!" little Neepy said. "Do you Raggedys know where the Strawberry-flavored Spring is?"

"No, where is it, Mister Neepy?" Raggedy Ann asked. "We have heard of lemonade springs and soda-water trees, but we have never heard of a strawberry-flavored spring! Have we, Raggedy Andy?"

"No!" Raggedy Andy replied, as he ran along beside Raggedy Ann and little Neepy.

"Do you know where the candy-covered cookie bushes grow?" little Neepy asked.

And when the Raggedys said they did not, little Neepy said, "Well then, I shall have to show you, for the Strawberry-flavored Spring is right in under the candy-covered cookie bushes, and as you sit and drink the strawberry-flavored soda-water, you can reach right up and pick the candy-covered cookies and eat them!"

Little Neepy ran through the bushes and under logs until he came to a thick part of the deep, deep woods, and the Raggedys ran with him.

Sure enough, there they found the bushes of candy-covered cookies.

JOHNNY GRUELLE

They crept in under the low branches of the cookie bush and there was the little Strawberry-flavored Spring.

The Strawberry-flavored Spring was as cold as ice—in fact, it was so cold that there were icicles all around on the grass at the edge.

The leaves of the cookie bush were shaped just like little drinking cups you see in the stores and all the Raggedys and little Neepy had to do, was to reach up and pick a cup and dip it into the Strawberry-flavored Spring, then reach up and pick the candy-covered cookies and sit there and enjoy themselves.

I wish that everyone could have a strawberry-flavored spring in his backyard and that there was a lovely cookie bush growing right over it.

"It all tastes so good, I wish Old Mister Gruffy Bear could have some, too!" little Neepy said. "Maybe the reason he is so ill-mannered is because no one has taught him to behave himself!"

"If Old Mister Gruffy Bear would be a nice Bear, it would be a pleasure for us to have him share the candy-covered cookies with us!" said Raggedy Ann.

"You two wait here, and I will run back through the woods and try and find Gruffy Bear!" said Raggedy Andy.

"All right!" Raggedy Ann and little Neepy said. "We will not eat any more candy-covered cookies, nor drink from the Strawberry-flavored Spring until you return with Gruffy Bear."

So Raggedy Andy ran back through the woods to little Neepy's tiny house.

And when he got there, he heard loud voices. One was Old Mister Gruffy Bear's voice and he said, "Don't you dare take those two little shiny red bicycles!"

"I guess I will if I want to!" the other voice said and Raggedy Andy saw that it was a Snoopwiggy. "I found the little shiny red bicycles here and they are not yours, so I guess I will take both of them. I need two bicycles to ride upon because I have four legs!"

"It doesn't make any difference if you have six legs!" Old Mister Gruffy Bear said. "Those two little shiny red bicycles belong to Raggedy Ann and Raggedy Andy, and if you take them, Raggedy Andy will wrestle you and throw you into the brook!"

"Pooh!" the Snoopwiggy replied. "Who's afraid to wrestle with Raggedy Andy, I'd like to know? He can't wrestle even a speck, I'll bet!"

"Ha! is that so!" Old Mister Gruffy Bear cried. "He can wrestle better than I can, for he threw me into the brook twice! And I'll bet I can wrestle you as easy as pie!"

"Huh!" the Snoopwiggy cried, real loud, "If you want to wrestle, I'll soon wrestle you into the brook for the third time!" And the Snoopwiggy ran at Mister Gruffy Bear and Old Mister Gruffy Bear ran at the Snoopwiggy and they hit together, "Blump!" The Snoopwiggy was a good wrestler for he had four legs and two arms, but that didn't keep Old Mister Gruffy Bear from throwing him right into the brook with a splash. "Now you can see who is the best wrestler!" Gruffy Bear laughed, "and I shall take the bicycles to the Raggedys so you can't have them!"

"I can catch you!" the Snoopwiggy said. "Just you wait!" But Raggedy Andy and Mr. Bear jumped on the bicycles and rode away leaving the Snoopwiggy to get out as best he could.

"You wrestled him fine!" Raggedy Andy told Mister Gruffy Bear. "I watched you all the time!"

"I wasn't going to let the Snoopwiggy take your two little shiny red bicycles!" Old Mister Bear laughed; "that's why I wrestled him!"

"I know it!" Raggedy Andy replied. "But what I can't understand is why you thought it was wrong for the Snoopwiggy to take our little bicycles, but you didn't think it

was wrong for you to try and take cream puffs away from Raggedy Ann?"

"Well, don't you see, Raggedy Andy," Gruffy Bear laughed, "when you threw me into the brook, two times, it washed me all off nice and clean!"

"Yes sir! You are a whole lot cleaner!" Raggedy Andy agreed.

"And that is just it!" Mister Bear said; "the water washed away every speck of Gruffiness and Grumpiness!"

"Oh goody!" Raggedy Andy said, "Raggedy Ann and little Neepy will be very glad! I came to take you to the strawberry-flavored ice-cold Spring, where the candy-covered cookies grow!"

"Whee!" old Mister Bear cried with happiness, "that's just what I like best! Candy-covered cookies and ice-cold strawberry-flavored soda-water!"

"And we will never call you Gruffy Bear again!" promised Raggedy Andy.

"How would it sound for you to call me Grinny Bear instead of Gruffy Bear? You see my initials begin with a G, so I must have a name which begins with the same letter!"

"I believe Grinny Bear will be a pleasant name, Gruffy Bear!" said Raggedy Andy.

"Now you see here!" Grinny Bear laughed, "just you call me Grinny Bear, Raggedy Andy, and leave off the Gruffy, because I don't care to be gruff or grumpy any more! It makes you feel inside all the time just like it was going to rain, or snow, or something, but since I am not gruff and grumpy, it makes me feel inside, just like a nice sunny day, with the birds singing and everything cheery and happy! It's a whole lot more fun than being gruff and grumpy!"

"I know it is, Grinny Bear!" Raggedy Andy laughed. "And I hope you never, never are disagreeable or ill-mannered again!"

"So do I!" Grinny Bear laughed. "Indeed, I shan't let myself get grumpy! If I feel the grumpiness coming on, I shall run and jump in the brook! That's what I shall do, Raggedy Andy!"

"You won't have to do that to get rid of the grumps and gruffiness!" laughed Raggedy Andy. "All you have to do, is just give your heart a 'sunshine bath' by saying, 'I love everyone!' "

CHAPTER THREE

THE SNOOPWIGGY AND THE WIGGYSNOOP

"IT'S a lot more fun being cheerful and kind than it is being gruff and grumpy!" Old Mister Grinny Bear said to the Raggedys and little Neepy as he came to where the Strawberry-flavored Spring bubbled up from the ground beneath the candy-covered cookie bushes.

"Of course it is, Grinny Bear!" Raggedy Ann laughed as she handed Grinny Bear a leaf-cup full of Strawberry-flavored Spring water. "Why do you ever doubt it?"

"Oh! I shan't any more!" Grinny Bear replied. "But before Raggedy Andy wrestled me into the brook, I was always grumpy and cross and gruffy! That is why everyone used to call me Gruffy Bear! But since Raggedy Andy threw me into the brook, I have felt so different it has been just like the golden sun peeping out after a black cloud passes by; that's how I have felt inside!"

"I guess it must have been a magic brook and that it washed away all your gruffy-grumps!" little Neepy said.

"No, it wasn't a magic brook!" a loud voice cried from the bushes, and here came the Snoopwiggy towards them.

"Oh, dear me!" Grinny Bear said. "Here comes the Snoopwiggy! I was hoping when I wrestled him into the brook, as Raggedy Andy wrestled me, that it would change Snoopwiggy as it changed me!"

"Well, it didn't!" the Snoopwiggy said, real mean-like. "And I am just as peevish as I was before. Now I shall chase all of you away from here, for I see these are candy-

covered cookie bushes! And that water from the Spring must be good, because you are not drinking it like water! You are drinking it like soda water, that's what! So you must all go away, or else I will start and chase you away! Then I will build a house right here and keep the candy-covered cookie bushes and the Spring all for myself!"

"We were here first, Mister Snoopwiggy!" Raggedy Ann said.

"What difference does that make?" the Snoopwiggy howled. "I want everything here all for my own, so you had better go before I begin chasing you away!"

"We shall stay right here, just as long as we want to!" Raggedy Andy said.

"I'll bet a penny, if I once start chasing you, then you'll go in a hurry!" the Snoopwiggy cried.

Raggedy Ann handed Grinny Bear and Raggedy Andy and little Neepy more of the Strawberry-flavored Spring water, but she didn't ask the Snoopwiggy to have any. "Now!" the Snoopwiggy cried, "just because you are taking some more of that Spring when I told you I wanted it all myself, I shall begin to chase you away!" But as none of our friends started to run, the Snoopwiggy scratched his head. "I guess I will begin chasing little Neepy first, then Raggedy Ann, then Raggedy Andy, then Old Mister Gruffy Bear!"

"Don't you ever, ever call me Gruffy Bear again!" Grinny Bear cried as he jumped up, "because I am not Gruffy any more, so now I shall wrestle you again!" The Snoopwiggy did not wish to wrestle again, but Grinny Bear just made him, and he wrestled the Snoopwiggy so hard, that in a few minutes, Grinny made the Snoopwiggy run.

Raggedy Ann and Raggedy Andy laughed to see Grinny Bear chase away the Snoopwiggy. The Snoopwiggy was a very selfish creature, for instead of being kind and generous, he wanted the Strawberry-flavored Spring and the candy-covered cookie bushes all for himself.

JOHNNY GRUELLE

"Whee!" Grinny Bear laughed when he came back to the Strawberry-flavored Spring, "did you see me chase away the Snoopwiggy? I'll bet he won't come back again!"

"We hope that if he does come back, he will be a better Snoopwiggy than he was before!" said Raggedy Ann. "The Strawberry-flavored Spring and the candy-covered cookie bushes are plenty large enough for everyone, almost, in the deep, deep woods, so no one should be selfish with them. They belong to everyone in the deep, deep, deep woods!"

"Well! Here I am again!" the Snoopwiggy cried, as he came through the bushes, and, with a stick, knocked lots and lots of candy-covered cookies down upon the ground. "And I brought my friend, the Wiggysnoop, with me so that you can't chase me away again. The Wiggysnoop and I shall chase you away, now!"

"Don't you believe it!" Raggedy Ann said. "And besides, it is wrong for you to knock the candy-covered cookies off of the cookie bushes and waste them!"

"I don't care!" the Snoopwiggy cried as he started to knock more candy-covered cookies down from the bushes. "If the Wiggysnoop and I can't have some of the cookies, then we won't let anyone else have any and will chase everyone away from here!"

"I shall take a stick and stir up the Strawberry-flavored Spring so that they can't drink any more from it!" the Wiggysnoop cried, picking up a stick and running toward the Spring.

"Now see here, Mister Wiggysnoop!" Raggedy Andy cried as he stepped before the strange creature, "it is always wrong to spoil anyone else's pleasure, just because you do not wish to enjoy that pleasure yourself! So if you try to stir up the Spring, I shall have to wrestle you!"

"Ha, ha, ha!" the Wiggysnoop laughed very loud, "did you hear that, Mister Snoopwiggy? I'll bet he can't wrestle worth two pins!"

"Don't you believe it!" Grinny Bear said. "Raggedy Andy is almost the best wrestler there is, I'll bet!"

"Pooh!" the Wiggysnoop laughed, "I'll bet he can't wrestle me at all!" And he caught hold of Raggedy Andy's arm and almost tore Raggedy Andy's pretty shirt.

Then Raggedy Andy took the stick away from the Wiggysnoop and wrestled him so hard he made the Wiggysnoop promise never to be mean again. Then he wrestled the Snoopwiggy and made him promise, too. Then Raggedy Ann gave them each a drink of the Strawberry-flavored Spring and a whole lot of cookies.

"Why!" the Snoopwiggy said, when he tasted the Strawberry-flavored Spring water and the lovely cookies, "this is so good that it is no wonder you did not want the Wiggysnoop and me to have it all to ourselves!"

"Such nice things should always be shared with others!" Raggedy Ann laughed, "for you will find out, Mister Snoopwiggy and Mister Wiggysnoop, that if you share your pleasures with others, the pleasures will seem ever so much better to you; 'cause, every time you give to others and make them happy, you catch some of their happiness, and that makes you just that much happier yourself! And the more you give away, the more you have yourself!"

"We have never tried that! Have we?" the Snoopwiggy asked the Wiggysnoop. "No!" the Wiggysnoop replied. "We always thought that the more you keep for yourself, the more you have! So we never have given anything to anyone else, and if we had a chance, we always took good things away from others!"

"My! My!" Raggedy Ann said, "of course that was being very, very stingy! And when one is stingy, it is just like shutting every door and window in a house and expecting the sunshine to come in! If you want to get real fun out of anything, just you try sharing it with another, then you'll see!"

"Do the Strawberry-flavored Spring and the candy-covered cookie bushes belong to anyone?" the Snoopwiggy asked.

"I guess they belong to everyone in the deep, deep woods!" Raggedy Ann replied.

"But if they belong to everyone in the deep woods, how does it come that all the creatures are not here enjoying them?" the Wiggysnoop asked.

"I do not know!" Raggedy Ann replied. "Maybe the Strawberry-flavored Spring and the candy-covered cookie bushes have not been here very long and not many people know of them!"

"Maybe!" the Wiggysnoop said.

"I tell you what let's do!" the Snoopwiggy said. "The cookies and the Strawberry-flavored Spring water taste so good, we should let everyone in the deep, deep woods know about them! So the Wiggysnoop and I will run home and get my horn and the Wiggysnoop's drum, and we will have a parade and tell everyone about the place, and invite them here!"

So the Wiggysnoop and the Snoopwiggy ran home and soon returned with the drum and horn. Then, with the Wiggysnoop and the Snoopwiggy in the lead, Raggedy Ann and Raggedy Andy and Grinny Bear and little Neepy had a parade.

CHAPTER FOUR

THE BANG GUN

IT WAS a very nice parade that the Snoopwiggy and the Wiggysnoop and the Raggedys and Grinny Bear and little Neepy had through the deep, deep woods. The Wiggysnoop had a horn and the Snoopwiggy had a drum and they made lots of noise so that the little creatures all ran out to see what it was.

"Is there a circus in the deep, deep woods somewhere, Raggedy Ann?" the little creatures asked.

"Oh, no! There isn't a circus," Raggedy Ann answered, "but there is a very, very nice surprise waiting for you down beneath the candy-covered cookie bushes! Just run down this path and take the first left-hand turn to the right and you will come to the candy-covered cookie bushes."

And the more little creatures our friends sent to enjoy the goodies, the more laughter and happy chatter the Raggedys and their friends could hear as they went along, for the little creatures enjoyed the candy-covered cookies and the Strawberry-flavored Spring soda-water so much that they danced and laughed, and they had so much fun it was just like a great big picnic party. Still the Raggedys and little Neepy and the Snoopwiggy and the Wiggysnoop and Grinny Bear marched along, telling more little creatures how to find the lovely cookies and the spring. Then, all of a sudden, they heard a real loud "BANG!" and the laughter and the chatter of the little creatures ceased as they raced in all directions.

JOHNNY GRUELLE '27

"What was that?" Raggedy Ann said.

"I'll bet a nickel it was a bang gun!" the Snoopwiggy said. "Let's all run and see who made the loud 'Bang!' "

So the Raggedys and the Snoopwiggy and the Wiggysnoop and little Neepy and Grinny Bear ran toward the Strawberry-flavored Spring. And peeping through the bushes they saw a great big fat man and in his hand he held a long gun.

"Hmm!" Raggedy Ann said as she and her friends stopped, "What shall we do?"

"I tell you what let's do!" the Snoopwiggy said. "This man has never seen a Wiggysnoop, or a Snoopwiggy, I'll bet, so the Wiggysnoop and I will chase him away!"

"What if he shoots you with the bang gun?" Raggedy Ann asked.

"Ha, ha, ha!" The Snoopwiggy and the Wiggysnoop laughed, quietly. "You just watch!"

So the Snoopwiggy and the Wiggysnoop slipped through the bushes real easy until they were right behind the man. Then they jumped out and howled as loudly as they could. Grinny Bear and the Raggedys laughed and laughed to see how the fat man ran away.

"What did I tell you?" laughed the Snoopwiggy as he started blowing his horn and the Wiggysnoop started drumming.

And soon all the little creatures came back to the Strawberry-flavored Spring and the candy-covered cookie bushes to spend the rest of the day enjoying themselves. "For," said Raggedy Andy, "the fat man was so surprised to see a Snoopwiggy and a Wiggysnoop, he will never come back, even to get the gun he dropped."

It was no wonder the fat man with the long bang gun ran, when the Wiggysnoop and the Snoopwiggy ran out in front of him and howled, for the Snoopwiggy and the Wiggysnoop were queer-looking creatures. And my! How they can howl when they want to.

Of course the Wiggysnoop and the Snoopwiggy mixed laughter into their howls, for the fat man was so frightened, when he saw the two strange creatures jump out in front of him, he rolled over and over many times before he got upon his feet and started to run.

"It served him right!" all the little woodland creatures said, when the Raggedys told them how the Wiggysnoop and the Snoopwiggy had frightened the fat man with the bang gun. "'Cause why? 'Cause! That fat man comes into the deep, deep woods ever so often and when his gun goes 'Bang!' then nearly everytime some little woodland creature gets hurt!"

"I do not see why some men like to do that!" Raggedy Ann said.

"Neither do I!" Grinny Bear said, "but they do!"

"Everyone with a bang gun that we see in the deep, deep woods, we will jump out and howl at! Won't we, Wiggysnoop?" the Snoopwiggy said.

"Indeed we will!" the Wiggysnoop replied. "I'll bet, if the Snoopwiggy and I had not been laughing so hard, we would have frightened him more than we did, for we can howl ever so much louder if we wish!"

"Maybe sometime we will ask you to howl real, real loud for us!" Raggedy Ann laughed, for the Wiggysnoop acted as if he wished to howl to show how loud he could howl, "But please do not howl now, because all the little woodland creatures are having so much fun, it might frighten them."

"All right!" the Wiggysnoop agreed. "We won't howl now!"

Just then Freddy Fox, who had run away when the fat man had shot the bang gun before, came running back to the Strawberry-flavored Spring as fast as he could run. Freddy Fox was almost out of breath, but he said, "Do you know what, Raggedy Ann and Raggedy Andy?"

"What is it?" the Raggedys asked.

"Why!" said Freddy Fox, "I was hiding under a log

JOHNNY GRUELLE

when I heard voices, and it was the fat man and another fat man, and they said they were coming back here to get the fat man's bang gun. You'd all better run!"

"Maybe we had all better hide!" Raggedy Ann suggested. So all the little woodland creatures ran and hid beneath logs and in hollow trees and beneath stones. All except the Snoopwiggy and the Wiggysnoop. They hid in under the candy-covered cookie bushes and waited for the two fat men. At first, the fat men did not think anyone was near the Strawberry-flavored Spring, but as soon as they walked up beside the Spring, the Snoopwiggy and the Wig-

gysnoop both jumped out, one in front of each fat man, and started to howl. My! How they did howl! Very much louder than they had howled before.

"Mercy!" cried the fat man who had been there first, "I never heard such loud howls! It makes my ears ache! I don't believe I want to get my bang gun!" And he and the other fat man ran away with their hands over their ears, and never, never came back into the deep, deep woods to bother the little creatures again.

When Raggedy Ann and Raggedy Andy left the happy little woodland creatures drinking strawberry-flavored soda-water from the Spring which bubbled from the ground beneath the candy-covered cookie bushes, they said to the Snoopwiggy and the Wiggysnoop, "Wiggysnoop and Snoopwiggy, we are so glad that you have changed from selfish creatures into nice kind-hearted creatures, we are going to give you our little magic bicycles. For the little red shiny magic bicycles run along ever so fast and you do not have to work your feet to make them go. We know you will have lots and lots of fun riding upon them."

The Wiggysnoop and the Snoopwiggy were very pleased to get the nice red shiny magical bicycles, but they said, "Thank you ever so much, Raggedy Ann and Raggedy Andy! But if you give us the two red shiny magical bicycles, won't that make Grinny Bear and little Neepy feel badly because they haven't bicycles, too?"

"No indeed, it won't," Grinny Bear and little Neepy said. "We think it is nice for the Wiggysnoop and the Snoopwiggy to have the bicycles! And we are very happy that the Raggedys have given them to you!"

"Oh!" Raggedy Ann hastened to say, when Grinny Bear quit talking, "It was very kind of the Wiggysnoop and the Snoopwiggy to think of Grinny Bear and little Neepy. It just shows that they have changed very, very much from selfish creatures into kindly generous creatures. But we did not intend to forget Grinny Bear and little Neepy. No sir! We gave the Wiggysnoop and the Snoopwiggy the two bicycles, and then we intended giving Grinny Bear and little Neepy, shiny red, magical bicycles, too!"

"Oh! Raggedy Ann!" the Snoopwiggy said, "how can you give away four shiny, red magical bicycles, when you only have two to give away?"

"Well!" Raggedy Ann laughed, "of course you do not know that I have a magical Wishing Pebble; a nice white one sewed up in my cotton-stuffed body! It's a secret, and all I have to do is make a wish and the wish comes true, right away! Doesn't it, Raggedy Andy?"

"Indeed it does!" Raggedy Andy replied. "And Raggedy Ann has a lovely candy heart, too, with the words, 'I love you,' printed upon it!"

"Then that's the reason the Wishing Pebble, which Raggedy Ann has sewed up in her body, works so well!" said the Wiggysnoop.

"So Raggedy Ann has a magical Wishing Pebble sewed up in her cotton-stuffed body, has she?" a gruff voice asked, and there stood a real tall man with a black cloak and a peaked hat. "I must have that Wishing Pebble, that's what! So hand it over to me!"

"How can she hand it over to you, when it is sewed up in her cotton-stuffed body?" Raggedy Andy asked.

The tall man did not answer. Instead, he jumped to catch Raggedy Ann, intending to take the Wishing Pebble away from her, I guess. But my! Didn't he get fooled? For he had only made one jump towards Raggedy Ann, when the Snoopwiggy and the Wiggysnoop and Grinny Bear made three jumps at him. "We'll teach you to bother Raggedy Ann!" the three good friends cried, and they pushed the tall magician, for that is what he was, this way and that, until they came to the brook, and then, splash, right into the brook.

CHAPTER FIVE

Hokus the Magician

THE Snoopwiggy and the Wiggysnoop and Grinny Bear ran back to where they had left Raggedy Ann and Raggedy Andy and Little Neepy. "Hurry!" Raggedy Ann cried. "Old Mister Hokus, the Magician, is climbing from the water and, my, but he is hopping mad!"

"It serves him right!" the Wiggysnoop laughed. "We won't let him take your magical Wishing Pebble, Raggedy Ann!"

The Wiggysnoop and the Snoopwiggy saw when they ran up to the Raggedys, that Raggedy Ann had wished for four more magic bicycles, all nice shiny red ones with rubber tires. "Quick!" Raggedy Andy cried. "Here he comes! Hop on a bicycle and follow us!" And the Raggedys jumped upon their magical bicycles and raced down the path in the deep, deep woods followed by Grinny Bear, Little Neepy and the Wiggysnoop.

Maybe you have never seen a Snoopwiggy, so I will draw a picture of one. You can plainly see that he is not the kind of creature to ride a bicycle. Maybe he could ride an old-fashioned "tandem bicycle," for a tandem bicycle is built to carry two people. And the Snoopwiggy having four legs, really needed a double bicycle.

If Raggedy Ann had only thought of this, then they would not have had such an exciting adventure as they had.

When the Snoopwiggy jumped upon the bicycle, only two of his legs had a place to ride and the other two just stood upon the ground and kept the magic bicycle from going even a smidgin.

The Snoopwiggy tried kicking his two back feet and finally made the bicycle go a little bit, but not fast enough. So, when old Mister Hokus, the magician, shook the water from his coat and ran after the Snoopwiggy, he had no trouble in catching him at all. "Ha, ha!" old Mister Hokus laughed. "So you thought you could get away from me, did you, Mister Snoopwiggy?"

And before the Snoopwiggy knew what had happened, old Mister Hokus pulled him from the magic bicycle and tied a string around his neck.

"It is a magic string and the Snoopwiggy can't pull away, no matter how hard he tries!" the Magician said.

Then old Mister Hokus jumped upon the Snoopwiggy's bicycle and rode home and the Snoopwiggy trotted along behind, for the Magician held onto the other end of the string. When old Mister Hokus reached home, he took the Snoopwiggy into his kitchen and tied him to the table leg. Then he tied an apron around the Snoopwiggy's waist and said, "Now then! I have always wanted a hired girl, so you can cook the meals and sweep the kitchen and brush

the crumbs away, just like Little Orphant Annie, but if you try to escape, then the magic string will pull you right back into the kitchen!"

"I don't believe that at all!" the Snoopwiggy said, as he ran out of the kitchen door, lickety-split. The Snoopwiggy ran out the door and almost across the porch, then the string jerked him back into the kitchen so hard he almost upset the stove.

"See?" Old Mister Hokus laughed. "Now you've got to stay right here in the kitchen!"

Maybe if the Snoopwiggy had not changed from a mean creature into a kindly creature, he would have been very cross when old Mister Hokus, the magician, tied him to the table leg with the magic string.

"When you set the table, you can get dinner ready!" old Mister Hokus said, and he walked into the other room and began reading the Sunday newspaper just as if everything was settled.

The poor Snoopwiggy didn't know what to do. He had never even fried eggs before, or made biscuits, but he knew he had to get the dinner some way or other because old Mister Hokus looked very hungry.

Magicians always look hungry, but the Snoopwiggy did not know this.

"Let's see!" the Snoopwiggy said to himself. "Maybe I had better fry him a dozen eggs and make some coffee!"

So he put the skillet upon the stove and placed six eggs in it and a lot of butter. Then he took a spoon and rolled the eggs around in the skillet. Finally one of the eggs grew hot and the shell broke right in two and the egg spilled into the skillet. Then another and another did the same thing until every egg was broken.

"Dear me!" the Snoopwiggy said to himself, "maybe he will be angry when he finds I have broken the eggs, so I guess I will put these away and get some new ones!"

So the Snoopwiggy scraped all the eggs into the fire and got six new ones. But these all burst open, too.

"This will never do!" the Snoopwiggy said. "They make the shells much too thin!"

Finally, after he had hunted all around, he found six nice shiny eggs. The Snoopwiggy thumped them and they seemed a lot harder than the others. So the Snoopwiggy put these in the skillet with a lot of butter and stirred them around a long time. These nice shiny eggs did not crack open like the others, for these were china eggs with which old Mister Hokus, the magician, April-fooled his hens.

When the Snoopwiggy thought the china eggs had cooked long enough, he put them in a saucer and put salt and pepper and sugar on them.

"Dinner's ready!" he called to the Magician.

Just as soon as the Magician saw the dinner the Snoopwiggy had cooked, he said, "My goodness, how do you expect me to eat that kind of dinner?"

The Snoopwiggy just shuffled his feet because he didn't know what to say.

"I'll go back and read my Sunday paper until you cook me something a lot better than glass eggs!"

"Dear me!" the Snoopwiggy said, as he sat down and crossed his four legs, "I wish he would magic a nice dinner, because he is going to be real, real hungry before I try to cook again." And leaning back against the wall, the Snoopwiggy was soon fast asleep.

When Raggedy Ann and Raggedy Andy and Grinny Bear and little Neepy and the Wiggysnoop jumped upon the magic bicycles which Raggedy Ann had wished for, the little shiny red bicycles carried them so fast, they did not look behind until they had gone a long, long way.

Then Raggedy Ann stopped and said, "Why, where is the Snoopwiggy. Didn't he get upon his magic bicycle?"

"I saw him jump upon his bicycle, just as I got upon mine," little Neepy replied. "But you know, Raggedy

Ann, the Snoopwiggy has four legs and maybe he cannot ride a two legged bicycle!"

"Oh! I never thought of that!" Raggedy Ann said. "We must ride back and I will wish for a four-legged bicycle for the Snoopwiggy!"

So they all got upon their little shiny red bicycles and rode back the way they came until they reached the brook.

"Here is where the Snoopwiggy and the Wiggysnoop threw the magician into the brook!" Raggedy Andy said. "And here are the tracks of the Snoopwiggy's bicycle! See! He tried to ride it, but his back feet dragged upon the ground!"

"And look!" the Wiggysnoop cried. "Here are the tracks of old Mister Hokus, the magician! I'll bet six and a half nickels, he captured the Snoopwiggy!"

"That is just what he has done!" Raggedy Ann said, "so we will follow the tracks and see where old Mister Hokus, the magician, has taken the Snoopwiggy. Who knows? Maybe he changed the Snoopwiggy into a pig, or something, with magic, when he reached his home!"

When Raggedy Ann and Raggedy Andy and Grinny

DELIVER
AT
REAR
JOHNNY
GRUELLE

Bear and little Neepy and the Wiggysnoop reached the home of old Mister Hokus, the magician, they left their bicycles by the back gate and tiptoed up to where they could peep into the kitchen.

There they saw the Snoopwiggy, sitting on the floor fast asleep.

"Psst!" Raggedy Andy said. But the Snoopwiggy was snoring so loudly he could not hear Raggedy Andy. Then Raggedy Andy tiptoed into the kitchen and awakened the Snoopwiggy. "Quick!" Raggedy Andy whispered. "We have come to rescue you from old Mister Hokus, the magician! Let's run out of the kitchen door as fast as we can and escape!"

"All right!" the Snoopwiggy replied, as he caught hold of Raggedy Andy's hand and started to run.

But the Snoopwiggy had forgotten that old Mister Hokus, the magician, had tied a magic string to the Snoopwiggy's neck and to the table leg, so when they reached the edge of the kitchen porch, the magic string pulled the Snoopwiggy back into the kitchen and upset a chair, and the Snoopwiggy kept hold of Raggedy Andy's hand and pulled him back into the kitchen, too.

"Aha!" the Magician cried as he ran out to see what had caused the racket. "So Raggedy Andy came to rescue you, did he? Well, well! Now Raggedy Andy is captured, too, for you will find that neither one of you can let go of the other's hand!"

When the Magician went into his parlor to finish reading the funny pages of the Sunday newspaper, Raggedy Ann and Grinny Bear and little Neepy and the Wiggysnoop tiptoed up on the back porch and peeped in the kitchen window. Then Raggedy Ann said, "We must think of some way to rescue Raggedy Andy and the Snoopwiggy!"

Grinny Bear and Raggedy Ann and Raggedy Andy and Little Neepy and the Wiggysnoop all sat down upon the Magician's back step to try and think of a way to rescue the Snoopwiggy.

They thought and they thought and they thought, until finally Grinny Bear said, "I know! I will run around to the Magician's front door and knock, then when he comes to the door I will cry, 'Boo!' so loud he will be frightened and run away!"

"Oh!" Raggedy Ann told Grinny Bear, "Just let me think a minute longer!"

After thinking a minute longer Raggedy Ann held her rag thumb over her mouth as a sign for all to be real still, then she tiptoed into the Magician's kitchen where the Snoopwiggy was fast asleep with the magic string tied around his neck and to the table leg.

Then Raggedy Ann took a knife from the kitchen table and cut the string from around the Snoopwiggy's neck. Just as she had finished doing this, old Mister Hokus, the magician, came in.

"What are you doing here in my kitchen?" he cried in a loud voice; so loud, he awakened the Snoopwiggy.

"I've come to rescue the Snoopwiggy, and Raggedy Andy, that's what!" Raggedy Ann said.

"Ha! Ha!" the Magician laughed real loud. "How can you rescue him when I have a magic string around his neck?"

"Because," Raggedy Ann replied, "the Snoopwiggy was asleep with his fingers crossed and I cut the string then. Everyone knows that magic doesn't work when you cross your fingers."

And of course the Magician knew it, too, so he said, as Raggedy Ann and Raggedy Andy led the Snoopwiggy away, "You have rescued the Snoopwiggy this time, but just you let me catch him again, and you never, never will rescue him."

But Raggedy Ann and Raggedy Andy just walked right away with the Snoopwiggy and left the Magician sitting in the kitchen biting his finger nails.

"What I would like to know is how you rescued me when old Mister Hokus, the magician, had me tied to the

table leg with a magic string, Raggedy Ann?" the Snoopwiggy asked.

"I just fooled old Mister Hokus, the magician!" Raggedy Ann laughed. "I pretended that if you had your fingers crossed, the magic wouldn't work, and because old Mister Hokus believed it, why, you see, it didn't work and so I just rescued you, easy as pie!"

"I'm very glad you did!" the Snoopwiggy said, "for I am not a very good hired girl!"

"A hired girl?" little Neepy asked. "How can a Snoopwiggy be a hired girl, when he is a Snoopwiggy boy?"

"That's just what I would like to know!" the Snoopwiggy replied. "But the Magician said that he had always wanted a hired girl to cook his dinners and brush the crumbs away and shoo the chickens off the porch, like Little Orphant Annie, and that he wanted me to be his hired girl! I tried to fry some eggs in butter, but just as soon as the eggs grew hot, the shells popped open and they spilled into the skillet, then when I found some real hard eggs and cooked them in butter, Old Mister Hokus, the magician wouldn't eat them because he said they were April-fool glass eggs he used to fool his chickens with!"

Raggedy Ann and Raggedy Andy laughed heartily at what the Snoopwiggy said, for, lots of times at home, they had seen Marcella's Granma put glass eggs in the nests so that the hens would lay more eggs to hatch into fluffy little baby chickens. And they had laughed when the Snoopwiggy had told of frying the real eggs and of the shells popping open.

"The next time you play hired girl, Mister Snoopwiggy," said Raggedy Ann, "you must put the skillet upon the stove, then put the grease into it, then break the shells of the eggs and drop the eggs into the skillet!"

"If you do that," the Snoopwiggy laughed, "then I don't see why it makes any difference if you just put the whole egg in and let it pop open!"

"Just because!" Raggedy Ann explained, "When you do that, then the shell gets mixed with the other part of the egg and it isn't good to eat! No one eats the egg shells!"

"I wish I had known that!" the Snoopwiggy said, "for old Mister Hokus looked ever and ever so hungry and I felt sorry for him!"

"Oh! you did, did you?" the Magician howled, as he jumped from in back of a tree and caught the Snoopwiggy. "Well then, you can just come back home with me again and fry the eggs!"

The Wiggysnoop and Grinny Bear wanted to wrestle old Mister Hokus, the magician, and take the Snoopwiggy away from him, but the Magician crossed his fingers and said, "If it was fair for Raggedy Ann to rescue him when he had his fingers crossed, then it is fair for me to capture him again, when he doesn't have them crossed!"

And of course Raggedy Ann and Raggedy Andy knew it was best to play fair.

"I wish that you had let me wrestle with old Mister Hokus, the magician!" Grinny Bear said to Raggedy Ann as they watched the Magician walk away with the Snoopwiggy. "I could wrestle him just as easy as pie, and I would have thrown him into the brook again and rescued the Snoopwiggy!"

"Well, but don't you see, Grinny Bear, when I rescued the Snoopwiggy from the Magician before, when he had the Snoopwiggy tied to the table leg in the kitchen, I told the Magician that the reason I could rescue him was because the Snoopwiggy had his fingers crossed. And of course, everyone knows when you have your fingers crossed, that means King's Ex. So, if it was fair for me to rescue the Snoopwiggy from the Magician when the Snoopwiggy had his fingers crossed, then it is fair for the Magician to capture the Snoopwiggy when the Snoopwiggy doesn't have his fingers crossed!"

"Yes, I know!" Grinny Bear admitted, "but just the same, the Magician should not capture the Snoopwiggy! It isn't any fun for the Snoopwiggy to be captured and made to cook eggs for the Magician!"

"I know what let's do!" Raggedy Andy suggested. "Let's follow old Mister Hokus and the Snoopwiggy to the Magician's home, and when he makes the Snoopwiggy cook the eggs, let Raggedy Ann wish that the eggs would pop open and burn the Magician on the nose, then while he howls we can rescue——"

"Why, Raggedy Andy!" Raggedy Ann said, "it wouldn't be nice to make a wish like that, because it would hurt the Magician to have his nose burned. It is such a long one!"

"Then," Raggedy Andy again suggested, "why not wish for something real nice for the Magician—something that will please him so much, he will forget all about wanting the Snoopwiggy to do the cooking for him?"

"Yes!" Raggedy Ann agreed. "That would be a much better way to work it! Now what shall I wish for?"

Raggedy Ann had to make the wish, because she had a magical Wishing Pebble sewed up inside her cotton-stuffed body and every time she made a wish it would come true, just like in fairy stories.

"Maybe old Mister Hokus would like a pair of roller skates!" the Wiggysnoop suggested. The Wiggysnoop was very fond of roller skating on cement side walks and that is why he made that suggestion.

"But the Magician said he wanted the Snoopwiggy to cook for him!" Grinny Bear said, "so the wish must be for something to eat!"

"I believe Grinny Bear is right!" Raggedy Ann said. "Suppose I wish for a lot of ice-cream cones and lolly-pops and chocolate candy and cookies and everything to be right on the table, waiting for the Magician when he gets home?"

"That will be lovely, Raggedy Ann!" the Wiggysnoop said. "And I hope the Magician asks us in to help him eat them!"

"Well," Raggedy Ann laughed, "then I will wish that, too!"

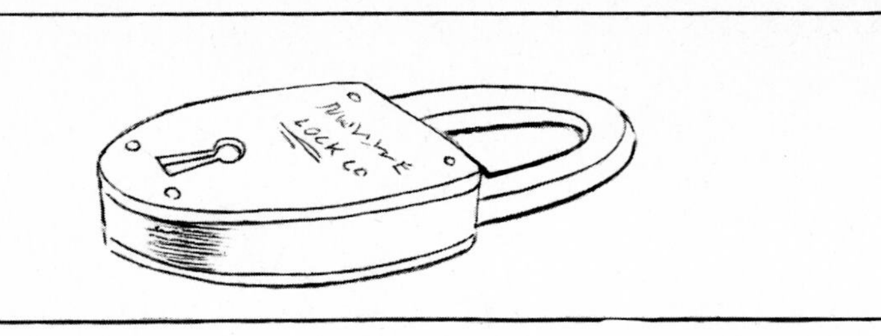

CHAPTER SIX

The Magic Lock

WHEN old Mister Hokus, the Magician, reached his home with the Snoopwiggy, he said, "Now I shall not let Raggedy Ann fool me again, as she did before! So instead of tying you to the table leg with a magic string, I shall put this magic lock in your pocket, then I will lock the lock and then I know you will not be able to run away for it won't make any difference even if you do cross your fingers, I've even got the King's Ex on finger crossing!"

"Then I guess I shall never be able to escape!" the Snoopwiggy sadly sighed.

"I just guess you won't," the Magician promised. "I never yet found anyone who could escape when I put the magic lock in his pocket and locked the lock. Even if I have never tried it, I know he can't do it!"

Old Mister Hokus put the magic lock in the Snoopwiggy's pocket and locked the lock. "Now just you let me see you escape, Mister Snoopwiggy!" the Magician said.

"I shall not try!" the Snoopwiggy replied.

"It wouldn't do you even a speck of good to try!" the Magician laughed.

"Aw! I'll bet I could escape if I wanted to!" the Snoopwiggy said, as they walked into the Magician's house.

"Huh! I'll bet a nickel you couldn't, even if you tried ever and ever so hard. Anyway, you must start right in and cook me something to eat, for I am getting hungrier and hungrier every minute and the longer you put off cooking, the more you will have to cook!"

The Magician tied an apron around the Snoopwiggy and put a spoon in one of his hands and a skillet in the other hand. "Now hurry!" he said.

The poor Snoopwiggy did not know what to do and was just about to sit down and try to go to sleep to forget all his troubles, when old Mister Hokus, who had gone into the dining-room, gave a glad cry and came running out. "You're the best hired girl I ever had!" he cried as he slapped the Snoopwiggy upon the back, "So take off your apron and come right into the dining-room and we will eat!"

The Snoopwiggy didn't know what to say, for he did not know that Raggedy Ann had made wishes for nice things to be on the Magician's table. So the Snoopwiggy just smiled and swallowed real hard and followed the Magician into the dining-room. There he saw the table piled high with goodies.

The Magician was just pulling up two chairs when Raggedy Ann and Grinny Bear and the Wiggysnoop and Raggedy Andy all knocked real hard on the door, THUMP! THUMP! THUMP! THUMP! like that.

"Ha!" the Magician cried as he ran to the door, "I hope that is company, because you cooked such good things and so many of them, I will have enough for six or seven people!"

And when he saw that it was Raggedy Ann and her friends, he cried, "Come right in and have dinner with the Snoopwiggy and me!"

And you see, that was just what Raggedy Ann had wished for, and it all came true, just like a fairy story. And, of course, all good things do really come true.

"Do you know!" the Magician said, as he pulled chairs up around his table for Raggedy Ann, Raggedy Andy, Grinny Bear, little Neepy, the Snoopwiggy, the Wiggysnoop and himself. "The Snoopwiggy is the best hired girl I ever had in my whole life, even if I never did really have a hired girl before! Why I tied an apron around him and gave him a spoon and a skillet and had hardly taken three steps until he had the table set and had cooked all the good things you see here!"

The Snoopwiggy chuckled as he passed the cream puffs to Raggedy Ann, "I expect, after all, Mister Hokus, Raggedy Ann must have fooled you again!"

"Ha, ha, ha!" the Magician laughed. "Don't you believe it, Mister Snoopwiggy! I have you fixed now so that you cannot escape! You see," he explained to the Snoopwiggy's friends, "I put a magic lock in the Snoopwiggy's pocket and I locked the lock—tick tock, like that—and he can't escape even if he wants to! So I know Raggedy Ann didn't fool me, for you are still captured!"

"Ho, ho, ho!" the Snoopwiggy laughed, as he passed the candy-covered cookies. "When you put the apron on me and handed me the spoon and the skillet, I was just about to sit down and go to sleep, for I do not know how to cook anything; then you came running back and slapped me upon my back and told me the table was covered with goodies!"

"And you didn't cook any of these things?" the Magician asked in surprise.

"Not even one of the lolly-pops!" the Snoopwiggy replied. "Can't you see Raggedy Ann and Raggedy Andy and Grinny Bear and the Wiggysnoop and little Neepy giggling and smiling? They surely must have fooled you again, Mister Hokus!"

"Well! if Raggedy Ann fooled me again, I'd just like to know how she did it? 'Cause she wasn't even in the house after I captured you the last time!"

"I see that I shall have to tell you, Mister Hokus," Raggedy Ann laughed. "When you captured the Snoopwiggy, the second time, we didn't know how we could rescue him, so we thought and thought until someone thought that it would be nice to wish all these goodies right on your table, for we knew the Snoopwiggy did not know how to even cook beans! So I just wished for all these things and here they were! Then the Wiggysnoop wished that we would be asked to have dinner with you. I wished for that, too! And when we knocked upon the door, you asked us all in to eat, and here we are."

"And it was very nice for you to ask us!" the Wiggy-snoop said.

"We like you ever so much better now!" Grinny Bear said, "For by asking us in you showed that you are growing kinder and more unselfish!"

"I had not noticed it!" the Magician said, as he passed the Strawberry short-cake with the whipped cream over it. "How does it feel to be kinder, Raggedy Ann?"

"Well, sir!" Raggedy Ann softly said, "have you ever pushed the petals away from a white rose and looked at the yellow center? It looks just like sunshine! And when you open your heart to others, it is just like that and your heart seems to shine with sunny happiness!"

"I really do believe that I am growing kinder and more generous," old Mister Hokus, the magician, said, "for when I first captured the Snoopwiggy and told him I wanted him to be my hired girl, I know that if he had cooked me ever so good a meal I would never have asked anyone in to share it with me!"

"I guess you were very, very selfish then!" Raggedy Andy said.

"I guess I must have been!" the Magician agreed. "And do you know? While I was mean and selfish, noth-

ing ever seemed to go right with me! I was always bumping my head, or falling down and hurting my knees, or stubbing my toes when I went barefoot! And then, too, when I was selfish, it seemed just as if everyone wanted to harm me and as if they were trying to do things to make me peevish!"

Raggedy Ann and Raggedy Andy laughed and so did Grinny Bear and little Neepy and the Snoopwiggy and the Wiggysnoop.

"Why do you laugh?" the Magician asked them.

"I'll tell you!" the Snoopwiggy said. "When we first met Raggedy Ann, she and Raggedy Andy and Grinny Bear were having lots of fun. Now I had always been just like you before, but something happened—I guess it was a touch of Raggedy Ann's magical candy heart, or something. And instead of being peevish and selfish, I changed and became kind and happy! So that even when you were unkind to me, I didn't even bite you once, or howl at you!"

"I didn't know Snoopwiggys could bite!" the Magician said in a surprised tone. "And you were so quiet, I never even once thought you could howl!"

"I can howl beautifully!" the Snoopwiggy said. "But not as nice as the Wiggysnoop can howl!"

"He can howl a great deal better than I can howl!" the Wiggysnoop said, "only the Snoopwiggy is too polite to say so!"

"Don't you believe it!" the Snoopwiggy laughed.

"If I had known that, I never would have captured you!" the Magician told the Snoopwiggy, "for I would have been afraid that you might bite me, and I would run like the dickens if you howled!"

"I shan't howl then!" the Snoopwiggy laughed.

"I guess just to be on the safe side, I had better unlock the lock and take it out of your pocket! For I am afraid you might forget and howl even if you don't mean to!"

"Do you mean that you will uncapture me, yourself?" the Snoopwiggy asked.

"That's just what I mean!" the Magician laughed. "You see, I really can't make a hired girl out of you, anyway, because you are a boy Snoopwiggy, and anyway, I feel so happy inside, I cannot bear to think of you being unhappy!"

"Then you will make me very happy if you take the magic lock out of my pocket," the Snoopwiggy said. The Magician did this and then said, "Now I will tell you a secret! I am not even a teeny weeny speck of a magician! I was just pretending it all the time!"

"And the magic lock wasn't a lock at all?" the Snoopwiggy asked.

"Sure! It was a lock!" the Magician replied. "But it wasn't a magic lock! 'Cause why? 'Cause I bought it at the ten cent store and anyone can buy as many as he wants, just like it, for ten cents!"

"Why not make a real magic lock out of it, just for fun?" Raggedy Ann said.

"How can we make it a magic lock, when it is only a ten cent store lock?" Mister Hokus asked.

"Well!" Raggedy Ann replied, "we can either pretend it is a magic lock, or I can wish it to be a real for sure magic lock. And, of course, if I wish it to be a real for sure one, then of course it will be. Because I have a Magic Wishing Pebble sewed up inside my cotton-stuffed body and every time I make a good wish it comes true!"

"Then do you mean for me to put the lock in the Snoopwiggy's pocket and lock it so that he cannot escape? You do not mean that, do you, Raggedy Ann? 'Cause I do not wish to make the Snoopwiggy my hired girl to cook my meals when he doesn't know how to cook!"

"Oh, no!" Raggedy Ann laughed. "I meant that I would wish it to be a real for sure magic lock and we could all take turns putting the lock in our pockets; then when we lock the lock, the magic would make it lock up our friendship forever and ever!"

"Raggedy Ann!" Grinny Bear cried, "that is a lovely thing to do and we will all love you for doing it!"

"All right!" Raggedy Ann laughed happily. "Then I make the wish that the lock will be a real for sure magical lock, and that whenever Mister Hokus wishes to make a friend, all he will have to do will be to ask the person to put the lock in his pocket, then, Mr. Hokus, you can lock the lock and you and the person will be good friends forever. When you have many kindly thoughts, it makes your life ever so happy; for each thought the friend wishes, of course you wish him a kindly thought in return."

"Then if I have a real for sure magical lock, I will really be a magician, won't I?" the Magician asked.

"Indeed, you will!" Raggedy Ann replied. "And if you will put the lock in our pockets, you will be a magician, right away!"

7-11
JOHNNY
GRUELLE

CHAPTER SEVEN

A Real Magician

RAGGEDY ANN could always think of the nicest things to wish for. Maybe it was because she had a candy heart with the words, "I love you," printed on it, and maybe it was just because she was stuffed with nice clean white cotton.

Raggedy Andy did not have a candy heart and, while he could not think of as many nice things, still he could think of quite a lot, and he was stuffed with nice clean white cotton, too.

So maybe it was because Raggedy Ann had both the candy heart and the nice clean white cotton stuffing, too, that she thought of the nicest things.

So Mister Hokus put the new magic lock in the Snoopwiggy's pocket and locked it, then in the Wiggysnoop's pocket and then in Grinny Bear's pocket and then in Little Neepy's pocket and then in Raggedy Andy's pocket and then in Raggedy Ann's apron pocket.

When old Mister Hokus put the lock in Raggedy Ann's pocket, he whispered to her, "I'm going to lock the lock two times so that we will always be two times good friends.

Raggedy Ann laughed as Mister Hokus locked the lock

two times and then she said, "Now I'll bet a nickel, Mister Hokus, that you are two times as good at magic as you were before! Just you try to magic something and see!"

"Won't it be nice, if I really am a magician?" Old Mister Hokus cried. "I can think of a great many nice things to magic already! First, I believe I will see if I can magic some ice-cream cones, for it has been almost ten minutes since we had dinner, and I know you must all be getting hungry!"

So Mister Hokus rolled up a piece of paper into a cone, little at one end and large at the other. Then he rolled up his sleeves and said, "I just wish to show you that I have no ice-cream cones up my sleeves!"

Then he took a little stick and tapped the paper cone three times, because that is a very magic number and said, "Hokus-pokus!"

Then he shook the cone in front of Raggedy Ann and out fell a nice strawberry ice-cream cone. Then in front of Raggedy Andy, and he received a lemon ice-cream cone. The Snoopwiggy and the Wiggysnoop each received a chocolate ice-cream cone and Grinny Bear and little Neepy a pineapple ice-cream cone.

"It's working fine!" Old Mister Hokus laughed. "You surely made a fine magician out of me, Raggedy Ann, and I thank you ever and ever so much! Now I will show you something else! See how short my beard is? Well! Real for sure magicians should have long beards! At least, all the magicians in fairy stories do. So I shall grow myself a real long beard."

So old Mister Hokus wiggled his wand in front of his face and said, "Hokus-pokus!" three times, and immediately his short whiskers began growing. "Look!" he cried after a moment. "They have grown two inches already! Now I shall soon have nice long whiskers, like I have always wanted!"

"Don't let them get too long, Mister Hokus!" Little Neepy said. "If they grow too long, you will look like a Billy-goat!"

"Oho!" Mister Hokus laughed. "I do not wish to look like a Billy-goat, so I shall let them grow three feet long, then they will be a lot longer than any Billy-goat's whiskers and I shall look just like a fairy story magician and that is just what I want."

Old Mister Hokus was very proud of the way his whiskers grew, and he walked to the looking-glass, every minute, to see how nice they were.

Finally, when his whiskers had grown until they reached down to his knees when he stood up, Mister Hokus stood in front of the looking-glass and asked, "Now! Don't you think they are just right, friends?"

"They are just right, now!" Raggedy Ann and Andy and Grinny Bear and little Neepy and the Snoopwiggy and the Wiggysnoop agreed.

"I think so, too!" old Mister Hokus proudly said, "So now I sha'n't let them grow any longer!"

Then he waved his little wand in front of his face and said, "Hokus-pokus!" three times. Still his whiskers continued to grow.

In fact, it seemed to hurry the whiskers more than ever and they grew until they touched the floor.

"Dear me!" old Mister Hokus cried, "What shall I do? They are much too long!"

"Why not cut them off just where you want them?" Raggedy Andy asked.

"I hadn't thought of that!" Mister Hokus said with a relieved sigh.

But when he cut a foot and a half from the whiskers, just as soon as he cut, the whiskers grew three feet. Then Mister Hokus cut his whiskers off near his chin. Immediately the whiskers grew twice as long as they had been before. Upon seeing this, old Mister Hokus began crying

and everyone felt sorry for him. For now his whiskers were more than two times as long as Mister Hokus, so that when he started to walk to the looking-glass, he stepped upon his whiskers and fell down.

Maybe it is a lot of fun being a magician and making ice-cream cones appear right out of a paper cone, but it isn't any fun to be in a fix like old Mister Hokus found himself. The whiskers were so long, Mister Hokus could not walk at all and there was scarcely room in the house for the whiskers and Raggedy Ann and Raggedy Andy and Grinny Bear and Little Neepy and the Snoopwiggy and the Wiggysnoop.

"What, oh, what shall I do?" the Magician cried.

"The best thing to do is to put the scissors away!" Raggedy Ann advised. "For you just make the whiskers twice as long each time you cut them off!"

"I know it!" old Mister Hokus cried, as Raggedy Ann wiped his eyes with her apron. "But I wanted nice whiskers just like all fairy story magicians have and I had no idea the magic wouldn't work properly! Can't you try wishing the whiskers away, Raggedy Ann, I do not care now even if I don't have any whiskers at all!"

"I'll try!" Raggedy Ann said, as she sat down in a corner of the room by herself and held her hands over her eyes. You see she had shoe buttons for eyes, and, of course, no one with shoe buttons for eyes can close them and wish real hard like real boys and girls can do.

"Now please, everyone be real quiet!" Raggedy Andy said. "For Raggedy Ann wishes to wish harder than she ever wished before, I guess!"

Raggedy Ann wished and wished for old Mister Hokus to have whiskers only as long as he wanted them to be. But although Raggedy Ann ripped four stitches out of the back of her head, where they didn't show, the whiskers remained the same length, but they changed from grey whiskers to an emerald green.

"Oh, how lovely!" Raggedy Ann cried when she took her hands from her eyes.

"Oh dear, oh dear!" Mister Hokus howled. "They are worse than ever before. Something must be done!"

But as no one could think of anything to do, they just sat there and wondered and wondered.

And after looking at the magician's green whiskers for a time, whenever they looked at anything else, even if it was white, it looked like red. If you look at a piece of green paper for awhile and then look at a piece of white paper, you will see what our friends saw.

CHAPTER EIGHT

The Witch's Magic

RAGGEDY ANN and Raggedy Andy and Grinny Bear and little Neepy and the Snoopwiggy and the Wiggysnoop all felt very sorry for their friend, old Mister Hokus, the Magician.

"Dear me! I do not know what to do!" Raggedy Ann sighed. "I wished just as hard as I could, but I seem to have made things worse!"

"The only thing I know to tell you," Grinny Bear finally said, "is that, deep in the center of the woods, there lives a Witch, and maybe if we go to her she can undo the Magician's magic!"

"Then we had better take poor Mister Hokus to the Witch at once!" Raggedy Andy said. "For pretty soon, if his whiskers continue to grow, they will be so long he will be unable to drag them through the woods."

"We had better start right now!" the Magician said, as he stood up and stepped upon his long whiskers and fell down again.

"I know what we will do!" the Snoopwiggy said. "I will take the first part of the Magician's whiskers and the Wiggysnoop the next part, and Grinny Bear the next part, and little Neepy the next part, and then Raggedy Andy the next, and then Raggedy Ann the next part. If we do not do that way, then someone will have to carry him!"

JOHNNY GRUELLE

And that is the way they arranged it. They made a queer looking parade as they walked along and the Magician felt very sad.

They walked and walked until they came to the Witch's little tumble-down house, and the Snoopwiggy, who was in the lead, knocked upon the door.

The Witch peeped out a chink in the door and when she spied who it was, she said, "Go away from here!"

"But we came to get you to unmagic the Magician's whiskers," the Snoopwiggy said.

"I know you did!" the Witch howled in a loud shrieking voice. "I shan't unmagic my own magic! I made his whiskers grow longer and longer on purpose, because I do not wish anyone else in the woods to use magic except me!"

"Then you are very selfish and unkind!" Raggedy Ann spoke, "and I am sorry that we came to you! We thought you might be a nice friendly witch. Instead you are unkind and selfish!"

"Don't you say that I am selfish!" the old witch howled at Raggedy Ann out of the window, "I'll make all of you have real long whiskers! That's what I shall do!"

"Then you will be meaner than ever!" Grinny Bear said. "And if Raggedy Ann will let me, I will come right in your house and bite you harder than hard!"

"Oh you would, would you?" the Witch howled, when she heard what Grinny Bear said. "Just for that, I shall grow whiskers on all of you, so there!"

And before they had gone twenty feet, Grinny Bear and the Snoopwiggy and the Wiggysnoop and the Raggedys had whiskers on their chins.

The Raggedys had yarn whiskers and they looked very funny.

"Whee!" Raggedy Ann cried, "Look at my whiskers! Just what I have always wanted all my life!"

And the Snoopwiggy and the Wiggysnoop and Grinny

Bear and little Neepy and Raggedy Andy all cried, real loud, "Whee! Look at our fine, nice whiskers! That was just what we wanted all the time!" And they winked at one another.

Now when the mean old Witch heard them shouting as if they were greatly pleased at having the whiskers on their chins, this made her very angry, for she did not wish to please anyone if she could help it.

"Dear me! How careless of me! I should have known that they came here especially to get whiskers like old Mister Hokus! Now I shall have to take the whiskers away from them again!"

And before the Raggedys and their friends had gone very far, they felt the whiskers disappear from their chins, and they looked at one another and winked.

Then the Snoopwiggy whispered to the rest and said, "Maybe if old Mister Hokus cries, 'Whee! I've got the best whiskers in the world!' and pretends to be glad because we haven't any whiskers, the old Witch will take his whiskers away from him!"

So they all walked back to the Witch's tumble-down house and Mister Hokus kicked up his heels and cried, "Whee! I've got the best and the longest whiskers in the world! If my whiskers were only two feet long, I would be unhappy!"

"Ha! What is this I hear?" the old Witch whispered to herself. "I must have made a dreadful mistake. I shall make his whiskers only two feet long so that he will be unhappy!" And she did this in just a few moments.

"Oh dear!" Mister Hokus cried. "Now I shall be unhappy for my whiskers are only two feet long!" And for fear the old Witch would catch on to the way our friends had fooled her, they hurried away through the woods, howling loudly as if they really were very unhappy.

But as soon as they were out of the Witch's sight, they all caught hold of hands and danced joyously.

"That was the time we fooled the old Witch!" Mister Hokus laughed. "Now if my whiskers would only grow white again, instead of staying green, I would look just like a real for sure magician!"

"Maybe, now that your whiskers are just long enough, if you work your magic you can change the color!" the Snoopwiggy suggested.

"Maybe I can!" the Magician said, "At least, I shall try it!"

So old Mister Hokus rolled up his sleeves to show that he did not have any colors up his sleeves, then he waved his little magic wand in front of his face and said, "Hokus, Pokus, I want my whiskers to be white instead of green! How do they look now?" he asked when he had finished working all the magic he knew.

"They are still as green as ever!" Raggedy Ann said.

"And they have started growing again!" Raggedy Andy cried. "They have grown at least a foot longer!"

"Oh dear!" the Magician cried. "I guess I should have let well enough alone!" And indeed, this is what he should have done, for his beard continued to grow and grow until it was ten feet long.

Tears came in the Magician's eyes and he would have cried, but Raggedy Ann hurried and wiped the tears away with her hanky—the one with the blue border. "It just goes to show that one should be satisfied when he has things fairly good!" the Magician sighed. "If I had not tried to improve on my whiskers, they would have been all right, for green is a nice color and it isn't eveyone who can have green whiskers!"

"No indeed!" Raggedy Andy agreed. "The only other person I ever heard of who had colored whiskers was Blue Beard! And just see how well known he was!"

"It will do no good returning to the old Witch's house, will it?" the Magician asked.

"Maybe it might!" the Wiggysnoop said. "Maybe we can fool her again!"

"No, you can't!" the Old Witch howled as she poked her head out from behind a tree. "I heard every word you have said, and I'll bet a nickel that you will not fool me again!" And laughing softly to herself, she waddled away through the woods, towards her little tumble-down house.

"I don't care, anyhow!" the Magician laughed. "I can wrap my beard around my neck in the winter time and it will keep me nice and warm! And just to show the old Witch that it does not make me very unhappy, I shall make a lot of magic goodies and we will have a picnic right here where we are sitting!"

And the Magician said a few magic words, and there upon the ground in front of them, appeared a table-cloth and upon the table-cloth was everything nice to eat you could imagine. So Raggedy Ann tucked the Magician's beard around in back of him and helped everyone to cream puffs, ice-cream cones and all the other goodies.

When they had almost finished eating, the Magician looked up and saw a little man standing over beside a tree looking at him.

"Hello, little man!" the Magician cried as he waved his hand to the little fellow. "Won't you come over and have some of our goodies?"

"Thank you very much!" the little man replied, as he came up to the magic table-cloth. "I was just wishing that I had something to eat!"

"Then you must sit down here with us and have everything you wish!" the Magician said, "And if there isn't enough, I shall make a whole lot more with my magic!"

"Oh! There will be plenty!" the little man replied as he sat down between Raggedy Ann and the Magician.

And indeed, there was plenty, for the Magician's magic worked fine except when he tried to change his whiskers. And the reason his magic did not work as well when he tried to change his whiskers, was because the old Witch's magic was stronger than his.

When the little man had finished eating as much as he wished, he asked the Magician if he had tried cutting off his whiskers.

"Oh, yes!" the Magician replied. "But whenever I cut any of them off, they grew just twice as long as they were before!"

"I see, then, that the mean old Witch has worked her magic on your whiskers!" the little fellow said. "But if you will come over to my house, I believe I can cut off your whiskers so that they will be just as long as you wish them to be, and no longer!"

"Can you work magic?" Raggedy Andy asked the little man.

"Oh, no!" the little fellow replied. "If I could, I would not have been so hungry when I stood and watched you enjoying the goodies here! But I know that there is a way to fool the old Witch and if you will come to my house, I will try it!"

"Maybe if you cut off the Magician's whiskers, they will grow twice as long as they are now, and then they will be twenty feet long instead of ten!" the Snoopwiggy said.

"I do not believe so!" the little man said as he led the way through the woods towards his house.

"If you can get rid of the Witch's magic she worked on my beard, I will make you a very nice present!" the Magician promised.

"Thank you very much!" the little man laughed. "But I do not expect payment for doing a kindness for another!"

"That is exactly how we should always feel!" Raggedy Ann said, "for, whenever we do a kindness for another, we always get much pleasure from doing it and that alone is payment enough!"

When this was done, and the Magician stood upon the ladder, the little man brought out a large pair of shears. "Dear me!" the Magician cried, when he saw the little man with the shears, "don't you know that if you cut my whiskers off, they will grow just twice as long?"

The little man laughed and then replied, "Please do not worry! I believe that I can fool the old Witch's magic! Now here we go!" And he took the ladder out from under the Magician so that the Magician hung in the air with his whiskers tied to the rope.

The Magician kicked and wiggled around a little bit, for it felt funny to find the ladder taken away from under him, but the little man said, "Please do not wiggle and kick so hard, for I may snip your chin if you move about!"

Then he reached up with the large shears and with one snip he cut right through the long whiskers.

As soon as the whiskers were snipped in two, the Magician tumbled to the ground and sat there feeling the remaining part of his beard.

"Whee!" the Snoopwiggy and the Wiggysnoop and Grinny Bear and Little Neepy and the Raggedys cried. "Your whiskers are not growing a speck, Mister Hokus!"

"I really believe you have fooled the old Witch's magic!" the Magician said to the little man. "How in the world did you do it?"

The little man laughed again as he said, "Well sir! Before, when you tried to get rid of the magic whiskers, you cut the whiskers off of you! But I fooled the old Witch's magic! For, instead of cutting the whiskers from you, I cut you from the whiskers!"

And indeed, this was true, for, there hanging from the tree were the Magician's whiskers and they had grown twice as long as they had been before; but this did not bother the Magician now, for the long whiskers were not hanging upon his chin as they had been before.

Raggedy Ann and Raggedy Andy were very happy when the little man had finished cutting the Magician off of his long whiskers.

"It isn't very nice to have such long, long whiskers!" the Magician laughed, "and I am so grateful to the little man. I shall work him a nice magical present!"

"My goodness!" the little man laughed in reply, "I do not expect anything in return for what I did! It is always a pleasure for me to do a kindness for another, and I do not want you to pay me!"

"I know just how you feel!" the Magician said, "but, please remember this: if it makes you happy to do a kindness for another, don't forget that it makes me happy to do something nice for another, too. So I wish to make you a magical present; and, if the present makes you happy, then, of course, it will make me happy, too!"

"Indeed! It will make all of us happy, too!" Raggedy

Ann said. "So, little man, please let the Magician make you a magical present!"

"If it will make all of you happy to see me get a very magical present, then, of course, I shall be glad to let the Magician give me something. But if I may have a wish, then I shall wish that the present shall be something which all of us may share!"

"Now I know that my magic will work well!" the Magician laughed. "For whenever I make real unselfish magic, it always is very good magic! So if you will tell what you would like me to make, I will make it just as quickly as I can!"

"I don't know what to wish for!" the little man replied. "Sometimes I have thought if I had a whole lot of things to play upon, like roller coasters and merry-go-rounds and swings and sliding boards and all those things, that it would be very nice. For then, I could let all the people who enjoyed playing upon such things come right into my place and enjoy themselves!"

"Do you think you could make so many nice things, Mister Hokus?" Grinny Bear asked.

"I can try!" the Magician replied. "You see," he explained to the nice little man, "I have not been a Magician very long! Raggedy Ann wished that I would be a Magician and her wish came true! But I do not know just how good my magic will work on real big things. So, first of all, I will magic some pop-corn balls and peanuts and red soda-pop; then, if I can magic the nice things you want, we can have the peanuts and pop-corn to eat, while we play upon the merry-go-round and other things."

So the Magician said "Hokus Pokus," and everyone had a sack of peanuts, two pop-corn balls, and a bottle of soda pop. Then he said "Hokus Pokus," sixteen times, and there was a merry-go-round, the sliding board, the swings and all the other things you usually find in a pleasure park.

So the Raggedys and the little man and the Magician and Grinny Bear and little Neepy and the Snoopwiggy and the Wiggysnoop took their goodies and played upon the merry-go-round and the other things until all the little creatures living nearby came and watched them. When the little man saw this, he said, "Let's invite all the little creatures to play, too!" And when they did this, the Magician made goodies enough for everyone who came to play. So you can imagine just how much fun everyone had.

And, while the Raggedys and the Magician and all their friends and the little woodland creatures were playing upon the merry-go-round and other things, and were laughing and shouting and having a lot of fun, Raggedy Ann looked over towards some bushes and saw the old Witch standing there watching them.

"Hmm!" Raggedy Ann said to herself, "I wonder if the old Witch is trying to make the Magician's magic quit working? For if she makes it quit working, all these nice things will disappear and the little man and the little woodland creatures will not have a thing to play upon!"

So Raggedy Ann hopped from the merry-go-round and ran over to where the old Witch stood. "Please, Missus Witch," Raggedy Ann said, "do not unmagic the Magician's magic, for if you do, you will spoil everybody's fun!"

The old Witch did not answer Raggedy Ann, because she couldn't. Her eyes were filled with tears and there was a lump in her throat.

Raggedy Ann took her nice clean hanky and wiped the old Witch's eyes. "Now I'll bet you feel better! Don't you?" she asked, as she put her rag arm around the old Witch's shoulder.

"I heard all the laughing and fun going on, so I came to see what it was!" the old Witch said. "And it made me feel very, very sad, when I saw what nice things the Magician had made for all the woodland creatures, to think how

hard I tried to keep the Magician from working his magic. So I just stood here and cried and cried!"

"Well! Don't cry any more!" Raggedy Ann laughed. "Just you come along and hop on the merry-go-round and see how much fun it is!"

At first, the old Witch didn't want to do this, but Raggedy Ann took her arm and pulled her right over to the merry-go-round and found her a seat upon a shiny white horse.

"Whee!" the old Witch cried, when the music started and the merry-go-round went around and around. "No wonder everyone enjoyed it so much! This is the most fun I've ever had!" And she laughed and yelled, just as happily as anyone else.

Then Raggedy Ann took her to all the other things and she enjoyed them as much as she had the merry-go-round. "Do you know what?" she said to Raggedy Ann, "after this, I shall never use any kind of magic except to bring pleasure to someone else, 'cause just look at the nice Magician. You can see that he is getting as much fun out of these nice things as anyone else!"

"Indeed, Missus Witch, that is quite true," Raggedy Ann replied. "If you just try it, you will soon find out, that whenever you do something kindly for another, you plant a seed inside your own heart, which grows into a happiness blossom, and, for every speck of fun you give another, you receive an echo of that fun yourself!"

CHAPTER TEN

The Magical Safety Pin

RAGGEDY ANN knew what she was talking about when she told the old Witch that every time anyone did a kindness for another it planted a seed within the heart which soon grew into a happiness blossom.

The old Witch said to Raggedy Ann, "It makes me feel sad when I see the merry-go-round and the other things the Magician made for the woodland creatures to enjoy. It makes me feel ashamed to think of the way I tried to unmagic the Magician's magic. So I shall go over under that big tree and sit down and try to think of something nice to give to the Magician."

"Maybe I can help you think of some nice things, Missus Witch!" Raggedy Ann said. "If you would like me to go with you, I will, and maybe I can think of something nice to magic, too!"

"Can you magic, too?" the old Witch asked.

"Oh yes!" Raggedy Ann replied. "But I am not a witch, nor a magician. I have a real for sure Wishing Pebble sewed up inside my cotton-stuffed body and almost every time I make a wish, the wish comes true!"

"It must be very nice to own a Wishing Pebble!" the Witch said, as she put her arm around Raggedy Ann and they walked over to the large tree. "Please tell me how you happened to get the real for sure Wishing Pebble! I

have looked and looked and looked for a Wishing Pebble, but I never could find one!"

"I found this one by the laughing brook!" Raggedy Ann said, as she sat down beside the Witch, "and lots and lots of times I have had mean persons try to take it away from me! But in the end, they all turned out to be nice, for, after they found out that there is always lots more fun in being kind and good than there is in being stingy and mean, they changed from mean to good. Then, of course, they did not wish to take the real for sure Wishing Pebble away from me. Instead, they were very happy to think that I had the real for sure Wishing Pebble!"

"And I am glad you have it, too!" the old Witch laughed. "If I had known it a short time ago, probably I would have wanted it and would have tried to take it away from you. You see," the old Witch went on, "the only magical thing I have is a left-handed safety pin, and while it works lots of magic, still there are times when it will not work magic at all!"

"May I see it?" Raggedy Ann asked the old Witch.

"Certainly," the old Witch replied, as she took the left-handed safety pin out of her pocket and handed it to Raggedy Ann.

Raggedy Ann looked at the left-handed safety pin and turned it over and over. "Do you know what, Missus Witch?" Raggedy Ann asked. "I believe it is a very, very good magical left-handed safety pin, but see here! It is bent, and I'll bet a nickel that is why you did not work good magic instead of unkind magic."

Then Raggedy Ann held her other hand over the left-handed safety pin for a moment and made a wish. Then, when she took her hand away, there was a right-handed safety pin lying beside the left-handed safety pin, and the left-handed safety pin wasn't bent even a smidgin.

"Now I'll bet a nickel," Raggedy Ann laughed as she handed the right- and left-handed safety pins to the old

Witch, "if you work magic, you will find that it is dandy fine magic, if you work it to give pleasure to another!"

"I'll bet so, too!" the old Witch cried. "And I thank you ever and ever so much, Raggedy Ann! Now I guess I will try and think of something real nice to magic for everyone here to enjoy!"

"Maybe if you would change the Magician's whiskers from green back to white it would make him happy!" Raggedy Ann said.

"Dear me! Has the Magician really and truly got green whiskers, Raggedy Ann?" the Witch asked. "I am color blind! And I can not tell green from red, or any other color!"

"Yes! His whiskers are green!" Raggedy Ann answered. "You see, when he tried to magic his whiskers and make them grow nice and long, you made his magic work lop-sided, I guess. Anyway, you made his whiskers grow so long he tripped upon them. Then, when I tried to unmagic his whiskers, your magic made them turn as green as grass!"

"Then I am sorry!" the Witch said. "And the first thing I shall magic is the Magician's green whiskers! But listen, Raggedy Ann!" the old Witch whispered, and she leaned over and talked so low, Raggedy Ann could hardly hear her.

But Raggedy Ann nodded her rag head and smiled as wide as she could.

"That will be a nice thing to do!" Raggedy Ann said,

out loud. "And I'll bet it will please the Magician very, very much, for I do not believe he would wish it for himself, for fear it might be a selfish wish!"

"Then I shall do it, Raggedy Ann!" the old Witch laughed. "Won't he be surprised?"

"You bet he will!" Raggedy Ann said out loud to the old Witch. Then, to herself, she thought, "And so will you!"

For you see, whatever it was that the old Witch intended doing for the Magician, Raggedy Ann intended doing for the old Witch. So the old Witch closed her eyes and held the right- and left-handed safety pins tight in her hands and made a wish. Then, while she was doing this, Raggedy Ann made the same wish for the old Witch.

"Has the magic worked?" the old Witch asked, as she opened her eyes.

"Indeed, it has!" Raggedy Ann laughed. "Just look at the Magician now!"

"It worked fine!" the old Witch cried, as she jumped up and ran to the Magician.

Everyone stopped their fun to look at the Magician and the old Witch. For you see, the old Witch had wished for the old Magician to be changed from an old man into a young man. And Raggedy Ann had wished, at the same time, for the old Witch to be changed from an old woman into a young woman. And both wishes had come true right away.

"Whee!" the Snoopwiggy and all the woodland creatures cried.

"Unselfish wishes are the best kind of wishes!" Raggedy Ann said, when she looked at the Magician and the Witch.

"If the Witch had not wished for the old Magician to be young and handsome, then Raggedy Ann would not have wished for the old Witch to be young and pretty again!" the Snoopwiggy said to the Wiggysnoop.

"I am glad that the old Witch made the kindly wish then!" the Wiggysnoop replied. "For it is lots more fun if everyone is happy! And I'll bet now the Magician will marry the pretty Witch, just like in real for sure fairy tales!"

"I hadn't thought of that," the Magician said, "but I think it would be nice!"

The pretty Witch thought so, too, and so did everyone else.

"Who will we have to marry us, I wonder?" the Magician asked.

"Why not let Raggedy Andy marry you?" the Wiggysnoop asked in reply.

"Oh! I do not know how to marry anyone!" Raggedy Andy said. "Someone else will have to do it!"

"Then I will be glad to marry them!" Grinny Bear said. "For I have watched a lot of weddings!"

"Whee!" the Witch and the Magician and all the woodland creatures cried. "Grinny Bear will say the wedding ceremony! Won't that be nice?"

"First, I must have a book to read out of!" Grinny Bear said, "then I must have a lovely ring for the Magician to put on the Witch's finger!"

"I will make a lovely book!" the Witch laughed.

"And I will magic a beautiful ring!" the Magician said.

It only took the pretty Witch and the handsome Magician a minute and a half to magic the book and the beautiful diamond ring and, as everyone gathered around in a circle beneath the great forest trees, Grinny Bear pretended to read aloud from the book and, in fifteen minutes, the pretty Witch and the handsome Magician were married.

While Grinny Bear was busy marrying the pretty Witch and the handsome Magician, Raggedy Ann's cotton-stuffed head had been very busy thinking nice things. And, because she had a Candy Heart and a Wishing Pebble sewed up inside her cotton-stuffed body, Raggedy Ann could easily think of happy things.

So, just as soon as Grinny Bear had finished marrying the pretty Witch and the handsome Magician, Raggedy Ann had thought out her wish and made it come true.

Raggedy Ann's wish was this, "I wish that everyone here had a lovely, beautiful wedding present for the pretty Witch and the handsome Magician!" And sure enough everyone there walked up to the pretty Witch and the handsome Magician and handed them the presents.

There were so many presents, when everyone had done this, the pretty Witch and the handsome Magician could not carry them all. So the Magician laughed and said, "Everyone will have to bring the presents and come to my brand new white marble castle!"

So while the birds flew above them and sang, the handsome Magician and the pretty Witch led the way through the woods to where the Magician had magicked the loveliest white marble castle.

CHAPTER ELEVEN

Magical Wishes Come True

"IT MUST be nice to own a Wishing Pebble, or a brass suspender button or a right- and left-handed safety pin!" the Wiggysnoop said to the Snoopwiggy as they went with the pretty Witch and the handsome Magician and Raggedy Ann and Raggedy Andy and Grinny Bear and little Neepy and all the woodland creatures into the beautiful white marble castle which the handsome Magician had made for the pretty Witch. "For with any of those magical things you can wish for such nice things!"

"I guess if I had any of those magical things, I wouldn't know what to wish for first!" the Snoopwiggy laughed.

Raggedy Ann was standing right behind the Wiggysnoop and the Snoopwiggy, when they were talking, and she thought to herself, "I'll bet it would be fun just to see what these two good friends would wish for, if they each had a wish to come true!"

So she said to the Snoopwiggy and the Wiggysnoop, "If you two might each make a wish and have it come true, what would you wish for?"

"I know what I would wish for!" the Snoopwiggy replied.

"Then," Raggedy Ann laughed, "I shall wish that you may both have a wish come true!"

"Now when I count three," Raggedy Ann said, "the Snoopwiggy shall make a wish!"

Then she called to everyone and said, "Just you all

watch and see what the Snoopwiggy is going to wish for, 'cause I have given him one wish which will come true! Then I shall give one wish to come true to the Wiggysnoop, so everyone must be real quiet, just like little baby mice!"

Of course, everyone was anxious to see what the Snoopwiggy and the Wiggysnoop would wish for, 'cause everyone felt sure that they would both make nice surprise wishes.

So the Snoopwiggy closed his eyes and wished, just as hard as he could.

When he opened his eyes, everyone shouted happily, for there right before everyone in the center of the handsome Magician's white marble castle hall was the finest ice-cream soda-water fountain anyone could wish for. It was made of white marble trimmed in gold.

"Thank you ever and ever so much, Mister Snoopwiggy!" the handsome Magician and the pretty Witch said. "It is a lovely soda-fountain and we must all try every flavor."

So all the woodland creatures and the Raggedys and Grinny Bear and the Snoopwiggy and the Wiggysnoop and little Neepy and the pretty Witch and the handsome Magician tried every flavor and all agreed that it was the finest ice-cream soda-water they had ever tasted.

"I think your wish was just as nice as it could be, Mister Snoopwiggy!" the pretty Witch said.

"Indeed it is!" the handsome Magician added, "for now, with a beautiful white and gold soda-water fountain, right in the center of our lovely white marble castle hall, we can have lots and lots of fun!"

"And everyone can come right in and have ice-cream sodas, whenever they wish!" the pretty Witch said.

"I am glad I thought to wish for the magical fountain!" the Snoopwiggy said, "for if you get a lot of pleasure from it, then that will make me happy, too!"

"Now!" Raggedy Ann said, "let us see what the Wiggysnoop will wish for! You know, I promised the Snoopwiggy and the Wiggysnoop that they could both have a wish which would come true!"

"Yes!" all the woodland creatures cried. "Let us see what the Wiggysnoop will wish for!"

"I shall wish for something which almost all boys and girls have wished for sometime in their lives!" the Wiggysnoop laughed. "I hope that it will please the pretty Witch and the handsome Magician, if my wish comes true!"

"Oh! we are certain it will!" the pretty Witch and the handsome Magician laughed. "Because it will be a magical wish and it is certain to be a nice one!"

So the Wiggysnoop closed his eyes, although he did not need to do it, and made his wish.

He was almost afraid to open them for fear his wish would not come true. But Raggedy Ann, because she had the magical Wishing Pebble sewed up inside her cotton-stuffed body, knew the wish, if it was a really and truly unselfish one, would come true. And sure enough it did.

When the Wiggysnoop heard everyone shout for joy, he opened his eyes and saw just what he had wished for.

At one side of the Magician's white marble castle hall was an entrance into the nicest and finest candy store Raggedy Ann and Raggedy Andy had ever seen, and they had seen a great many.

All the candy in the magical candy store was in neat white glass dishes and each dish was filled with a different kind of candy, chocolates and cream candies and every kind. There were even licorice candies!

"And I wished that each time one of the candy dishes was emptied, that it would fill right up again!" the Wiggysnoop said, as everyone walked into the lovely place and started eating candy.

And of course, when the Raggedys and the Magician and the pretty Witch and their friends heard the Wiggysnoop say this, they knew he had spent a lot of time thinking out his wish. And, of course, it was a wish which every boy and girl has made sometime in his life. And you may be sure, the handsome Magician and his pretty Witch wife were very happy to receive such lovely presents with which they could make others happy.

All the time the Wiggysnoop and the Snoopwiggy were making their wishes, Raggedy Andy had noticed the dancing of Grinny Bear's eyes. "He is just as happy as if they had been his magical wishes!" Raggedy Andy thought. Then he walked over to Raggedy Ann and whispered, "Don't you think it would be nice for you to give nice old Grinny Bear a wish, too, Raggedy Ann?"

Raggedy Ann laughed, as she answered, "Don't you think that I had forgotten Grinny Bear, Raggedy Andy! I shall let him make his wish now!"

Then she called to Grinny Bear, "Oh Grinny Bear!" she said, "I have saved your wish until now! So you make a wish and have it come true!"

"Thank you, dear Raggedy Ann!" Grinny Bear said. "While I did not expect to make a wish, still I have thought of one!"

"Now we must all remain quiet while Grinny Bear makes his wish!" the handsome Magician laughed.

So everyone gathered around Grinny Bear in the great hall of the Magician's castle and Grinny Bear made his wish.

When Grinny Bear opened his eyes and smiled around at everyone, everyone turned around and looked about the great hall of the castle. Maybe they expected Grinny Bear to wish for another candy store, or another soda-water fountain.

"Now what in the world did you wish for, Grinny Bear?" everyone asked in a jumble of voices.

"We will have to go outside to see if my wish has come true!" Grinny Bear laughed. "My! I hope it has!"

So everyone ran to the great doors of the castle and looked out and when they looked out, they all had to hold their breaths in amazement.

"I knew it!" Raggedy Ann cried, her happiness making her shoe-button eyes almost jiggle off their threads. "Grinny Bear has thought his gift out to the last detail!"

The pretty Witch and the handsome Magician caught Grinny Bear and hugged him tightly, even though he wiggled and tried to get away, for this is what they saw, when they looked out of the great doors of the castle.

The castle, instead of being upon the flat ground, as it had been before, now stood upon a high island entirely surrounded with lovely blue water; pretty boats, just like beautiful birds, were sailing around far below.

And at one side of the castle was the merry-go-round and all the other wonderful things in which to have fun,

and at the other side of the castle were little houses of white marble with red roofs. And over the door of each, on a neat little sign, was the name of the woodland creature who should live there. Everyone walked around looking at the pretty houses.

"Yes, sir, Mister Grinny Bear! You have made a wonderful wish!" the pretty Witch said. "Now we can all live here happily, forever and ever just as if we were all in Fairyland!"

"Now dear little Neepy must have a wish!" Raggedy Ann said. "Have you thought of one, little Neepy?"

"I shall just wish that all of us may live here, loving each other and sharing each other's pleasures!" little Neepy said in a quiet voice. "And that this lovely place shall be invisible to all who travel through the deep, deep woods, excepting to those who have kindly, generous hearts, or to those who are in trouble and need our assistance. And"—little Neepy smiled to think of how much he was wishing at one time—"that a little white magic boat shall always meet those who visit us and bring them to our lovely island!"

"That is a beautiful wish, little Neepy," everyone cried.

Then the Wiggysnoop and the Snoopwiggy threw their hats in the air and howled ever so loudly, "Let us make little Neepy our King! Long live King Neepy!"

"Oh no!" little Neepy cried, when the two friends had stopped howling. "No one should be King! We must all be just like brothers and sisters and no one any better than another!"

"Little Neepy is quite right!" Raggedy Ann laughed.

You may be certain that the pretty Witch, the handsome Magician and the Snoopwiggy and the Wiggysnoop and Grinny Bear and little Neepy and all the woodland creatures were as happy as could be. They all cried, "Three cheers for Raggedy Ann and Raggedy Andy!"

"I know what we should do!" the handsome Magician

said, "We should name our place 'Raggedy Island,' so that whoever comes to share our happiness and pleasures will know that Raggedy Ann and Raggedy Andy have made it possible!"

The pretty Witch hugged Raggedy Andy and the Magician hugged Raggedy Ann and afterwards all the others hugged them, too, and said, "We shall always love you!"

And the Raggedys replied, "And we shall always love you, too!"

Then Raggedy Ann felt of her cotton-stuffed body and everyone looked at her.

"What is the trouble, Raggedy Ann?" Raggedy Andy asked, as he ran to her side.

"Oh! We hope Raggedy Ann is not going to be ill!" the little woodland creatures cried.

"Oh no!" the pretty Witch said, "Raggedy Ann cannot be ill! But tell us, dear Raggedy Ann!"

"It's the magical Wishing Pebble!" Raggedy Ann replied. "It is jiggling around in my cotton-stuffed body, and I am sure it wishes me to know something!"

"Now we must all remain very quiet, while Raggedy Ann wishes to know why the magical Wishing Pebble jiggles!" Raggedy Andy said, as he held up his rag hand for silence.

Everyone remained quiet while Raggedy Ann covered her shoe-button eyes with her hands.

Then, when she took her hands away, everyone could see that both shoe-button eyes were quite wet.

"I am sorry in one way, and happy in another!" Raggedy Ann said in her soft cottony voice. "Raggedy Andy and I must leave at once! Marcella has reached home and, remembering that she left Raggedy Andy and me in the little play-house out in the garden, she is anxious to find us there, safe and sound! The time is short, we cannot even kiss you all goodby, but you must know how much we shall always love you!"

And Raggedy Ann caught hold of Raggedy Andy's hand and, covering her eyes, she made the wish to be in the play-house immediately.

And, as she and Raggedy Andy found themselves there, they seemed to hear a faint chorus of all their friends crying, "And we shall always love YOU!"

But Raggedy Ann and Andy had no time to say anything, for Marcella was running down the path through the orchard, as fast as she could run.

She threw aside the door covering and caught the two loppy rag dolls in her arms and as she ran up towards the house with them she said, "I forgot and left you there until mama and I were almost in town, then it was too late, but, oh dear, I was afraid something would happen to you." Then she laughed softly, "And I had all my fright for nothing, Mama," as she walked into the house. "The dear old Raggedys had not moved at all, all the time we were away!"

And Raggedy Ann and Raggedy Andy wiggled their shoe-button eyes at each other, as much to say, "Ha, ha, ha! Is that so?"

THE END

RAGGEDY ANN
in the
MAGIC BOOK

WORTH GRUELLE

RAGGEDY ANN in the MAGIC BOOK

Written by JOHNNY GRUELLE

Illustrated by his son WORTH

To Uncle Johnny

Chapter One

THE Deep, Deep, Woods always filled with cool, blue-green shadows and patches of golden, sparkling sunlight is surely a wonderful place for fairies, elves, gnomes and magical, teeny weeny creatures to live.

Raggedy Ann and Raggedy Andy each with a rag arm around the other's shoulder, stood for a moment listening to the gentle whispering of the wind through the hemlocks.

"Let us follow the Tumbling Brook!" Raggedy Andy suggested, "We will surely meet with wonderful adventures along its mossy banks. And we shall enjoy its cheery, tinkling, laughter, as we go along."

"Yes!" agreed Raggedy Ann, "Let us follow the tinkling, tumbling, laughing brooklet."

So, the two kindly rag dolls, their cotton stuffed heads filled with pleasant thoughts, walked along the mossy bank of the tumbling brooklet until they met a funny little creature who said he was a Fuzzywump.

The Fuzzywump was really a very comical looking little weezy-wuzzy Fuzzywump, and always did just the opposite of what he said he would do, so that strangers like the Raggedys were fooled a lot before they found this to be true.

"Very disagreeable morning!" the Fuzzywump said as the two kindly rag dolls walked up to him. "What are your names?"

"Good morning!" the Raggedys laughed, "Our names are Raggedy Ann and Raggedy Andy."

"Funny names!" said the Fuzzywump; meaning, he thought they were very nice names. "My name is just Fuzzywump, which is a very, very lovely name." The Fuzzywump meant by this, he did not like the name. "We think it is a very nice name, too!" said Raggedy Ann with her cheeriest smile.

"That is the first time anyone has ever told me so," the Fuzzywump cried. "My house is just beyond the clump of ferns." The Fuzzywump led the way to a cunning little house nestling beneath the cuddling branches of a great tree.

When they reached the cute little house, the Fuzzywump opened the door, walked inside, said, "Come in!" and then closed and locked the door behind him.

"HMMM!" the Raggedys mused as their shoe button eyes twinkled in merriment, "How funny! he asks us in then locks the door so that we may not enter!" But, they did not say this out loud.

Instead Raggedy Andy said, "I do not believe we can come in today, Mister Fuzzywump! We will go on!"

Then the Fuzzywump opened the door, caught the Raggedys by their hands and pulled them inside saying, "Stay out of my cunning little house. I do not like to have visitors."

The Fuzzywump meant by this, he *DID* like to have visitors, but the Raggedys did not know it, and looked at each other with wonderment in their shoe button eyes.

"I never have had a dog," the Fuzzywump continued, "And, I hope that I never own one, especially a cross eyed puppydog."

The Fuzzywump went to a little box in the corner of the room and opened it. A little brown dog with crossed eyes popped out of the box and ran to the Raggedys, wagging his tail with pleasure.

"We will have nothing to eat today!" said the Fuzzywump as he placed a nice lunch on the table.

"What a queer little creature!" Raggedy Ann whispered to Raggedy Andy, "Let's stay, just for fun," and she pulled her chair up to the table. Raggedy Andy did the same, and the puppydog winked his "crossest" eye at the Raggedys, as if to say, "The Fuzzywump is just fooling you."

When the Fuzzywump had finished eating, he said, "I shall not stir out of the house today." And, with that, he walked out the front door. Then poking his head back inside, he said to the Raggedys, "Sit perfectly quiet! Do not move from your chairs! Don't touch a thing! Do not look

WORTH
GRUELLE

at my picture books, nor play the organ! Do not go to the cupboard and eat anything!"

When the Fuzzywump had walked down the path out of sight, Raggedy Andy turned in his chair and said to Raggedy Ann, "He said he would not stir out of the house today, and now, he has gone."

The little puppydog was only four inches high and as cunning a little creature as you can imagine. He sat on the floor and winked his "crossest" eye.

The Raggedys watched the funny little clock on the mantel for two hours and never once stirred from their chairs, for, you know, rag dolls can be very, very patient.

Finally the little puppydog spoke so suddenly, Raggedy Andy tumbled backward out of his chair, for neither of the Raggedys knew the puppydog could talk. "Why don't you get up and look about the Fuzzywump's little house?"

Raggedy Ann smiled her cheery smile and Raggedy Andy picked himself from the floor. "But, the Fuzzywump told us not to move from our chairs," the Raggedys both cried.

The little puppydog thumped the floor with his tail and chuckled, "If you stay here awhile, you will learn that the Fuzzywump says just the opposite of what he truly means, and when he said for you not to stir from your chairs, he meant that you should look about and make yourselves perfectly at home."

"How funny!" Raggedy Ann laughed.

"Yes!" the puppydog agreed, "when the Fuzzywump tells you to do one thing, it is because he wishes you to do another, just the opposite."

"We will remember!" Raggedy Ann smiled.

"Look in that large book on the mantel!" the puppydog suggested.

Raggedy Andy lifted the book from the shelf and he, Raggedy Ann, and the puppydog sat upon the floor.

Raggedy Andy opened the book, "Why, there is nothing in the book but blank pages!"

"Ha, ha, ha!" the puppydog laughed, "Don't you fool yourself. It's a very magical book and you turned the pages too fast."

"Then I'll turn the pages slowly!" said Raggedy Andy.

At first, the pages were blank, then there came a faint green spot. This grew just as a sprout grows out of the ground, only very much faster. As they watched, the sprout grew into a vine, and the vine grew until it covered the entire page. Raggedy Andy turned the page and the vine had grown on to this page, too. And, as they watched, the Raggedys and the puppydog saw a boy walk up to the vine and start to climb it.

"It's Jack and the Bean Stalk!" the puppydog shouted as he thumped the floor with his tail.

Jack climbed the bean stalk until he reached the top. There he stood upon a road and at the end of the road was a great castle.

"Now Jack is walking down the road to the castle," the puppydog cried. "And he's knocking upon the great door with his stick," Raggedy Ann said, "Look! an old woman has opened the door, and Jack is going inside. I hope the giant does not catch him."

Raggedy Andy turned the page of the magic book so that he, Raggedy Ann, and the puppydog could see everything happen just as if they were sitting at the movies.

They saw the old woman give Jack something to eat. Saw her hide him in a great iron pot when the giant came stomping into the room, and watched through the entire story until the giant started to chase Jack, after Jack had taken the giant's magic singing harp. Then, when the giant ran after Jack and was about to catch him, Raggedy Andy grew so excited, he lost his balance and fell right into the magical book.

Now, if the Fuzzywump's book had not been a magical book, Raggedy Andy could not have fallen into it, but, being a magical book, Raggedy Andy not only fell into the book, but he fell right in the roadway a short distance in front of the giant.

The giant picked Raggedy Andy up and shook him. "A HA!" the giant cried, "Now I have caught you!"

Of course, no one knows what might have happened to Raggedy Andy if the puppydog had not jumped into the magic book and nipped the heels of the giant. "Ouch!" the giant cried as he dropped Raggedy Andy, "I shall not stay here and have my heels nipped by a puppydog." And he ran for his castle lickity-split and banged the door behind him.

Raggedy Ann reached into the magic book and lifted Raggedy Andy and the puppydog out. "My goodness! I thought you were in for it that time, Raggedy Andy!" the puppydog said.

"So did I!" Raggedy Andy laughed as he patted the puppydog's head, "Thank you for rescuing me."

"Maybe we had better not look at the magical book until the Fuzzywump returns," the puppydog suggested, "For, the book did not work right for us and we might get into trouble."

"Yes!" Raggedy Andy agreed, as he took the magical book back to the mantel, "We will wait until the Fuzzywump returns."

When the Fuzzywump returned, Raggedy Ann said, "We have had a lot of fun while you were away."

"I am very, very sorry," the Fuzzywump replied, and of course, he meant he was very, very glad.

If the puppydog had not told the Raggedys of the Fuzzywump's queer way of talking, the Raggedys would have thought the Fuzzywump to be very rude.

"We looked at your magic book while you were away," Raggedy Ann told the Fuzzywump, "And, it was so exciting, Raggedy Andy fell into the book and was picked up by the giant."

"He intended taking me to his castle and shutting me up in an iron box," Raggedy Andy said.

"I am very sorry he didn't," the Fuzzywump grumbled.

The little puppydog winked his crossest eye at the Raggedys and said, "But, I jumped into the book and nipped the giant on the heel and rescued Raggedy Andy."

"Then, I must punish you," the Fuzzywump cried as he gave the puppydog a cookie and patted his head.

"I understand perfectly why the magic book worked so well for you," the Fuzzywump said as he took the book from the mantel. "Did you open it this way, Raggedy Andy?"

"No!" Raggedy Andy answered, "I opened it the other way!" "Then I understand why you got into trouble!" The Fuzzywump said. But by the puzzled look on his face, the Raggedys knew he meant he could not understand.

"We will not look in the magic book any more today," the Fuzzywump said as he opened the book. Raggedy Ann, Raggedy Andy and the puppydog sat on the floor beside the Fuzzywump and watched.

"I am so glad it isn't Cinderella," the Fuzzywump said as Cinderella appeared in the book, sitting near a fireplace watching a pot boiling above the coals.

"Look!" the puppydog cried, "There are the two mean stepsisters of Cinderella."

The two stepsisters slapped Cinderella and tweaked her ears.

At this, Raggedy Ann caught the two mean sisters and lifted them right out of the book. "Aren't you ashamed of yourselves!" Raggedy Ann exclaimed, "Cinderella is so pretty, you should love her instead of mistreating her as you do."

"Do not put them back in the book!" the Fuzzywump commanded, "We do not care to see how Cinderella marries the handsome prince and the story turns out with happiness for all."

Raggedy Ann knew the Fuzzywump wished her to return the sisters to the book, so she put them down beside Cinderella.

The two sisters looked frightened and hurried from the room as fast as they could go. "I am afraid you have not mixed up the story," the Fuzzywump said to Raggedy Ann as a nice looking prince walked into the kitchen and placed a tiny glass slipper on Cinderella's foot. Then there came a loud bump at the door, a large pumpkin rolled toward

Cinderella and upset the prince. As he fell, the prince kicked a hole in the pumpkin and sixteen mice ran out.

With a loud bark, the puppydog jumped into the magic book and chased the mice. Cinderella upset the pot and spilled soup all over the prince's fine clothes, just as the sisters ran in with brooms.

The mice changed into snow white horses and went galloping out the door just as a queer little old woman came in.

The puppydog chased after the horses, and when the queer little old woman smoothed out her clothes and sat up, the puppydog came bouncing back into the room, wagging his tail just as if he had done something wonderful.

The Fuzzywump slammed the book shut and said, "That was fine! exactly as the story goes. If Raggedy Ann had kept her hands out of the book everything would have gone wrong. Now, I haven't lost my little cross eyed puppydog, and I am happy." And with this, the funny Fuzzywump took out his pocket hanky and laughed, and laughed into it.

Raggedy Ann and Raggedy Andy knew the Fuzzywump meant just the opposite of what he said, so, Raggedy Ann

took the book from him and opened it. There she saw the queer little old woman, the two sisters, and the prince chasing the puppydog around the room.

Raggedy Ann reached into the magic book and lifted the puppydog out. "Goodness me!" the puppydog said when he caught his breath, "Did you ever see such cross people in all your life? They didn't seem a bit pleased because I chased the lovely white horses."

When the Fuzzywump saw that Raggedy Ann had rescued the puppydog, the Fuzzywump put his hanky in his pocket and cried as if his heart would break. The puppydog licked the Fuzzywump's hand and wagged his stubby little tail with joy.

"Oh, dear!" the Fuzzywump wailed, "The puppydog is back again and I am so disappointed and unhappy."

"You are just putting this all on!" Raggedy Andy cried as he caught the heels of the Fuzzywump and turned him upside down. "Maybe this will straighten everything out so you will not say everything upside down." And Raggedy Andy bounced the Fuzzywump up and down.

When Raggedy Andy dropped him to the floor, the

Fuzzywump sat up and rubbed his head. "What has happened?" he asked.

Raggedy Andy told the Fuzzywump what he had done.

"Well! well!" the Fuzzywump mused, "You say that I have been saying just the opposite of what I meant!"

"For years and years!" the puppydog answered.

"Then, I thank Raggedy Andy," the Fuzzywump said, and meant every word. "So, I shall give him a present."

Raggedy Andy thought the Fuzzywump was fooling again, for he went to a cupboard and came back with a little crooked stick. "It is yours!" he said as he handed it to Raggedy Andy.

"How did you ever get the habit of saying exactly the opposite of what you mean?" Raggedy Ann asked the Fuzzywump.

"It is a sad, sad story!" the Fuzzywump replied as he went to the cupboard and returned with a large dish of chocolate ice cream.

"I will tell you as soon as I dish out this ice cream. The cross eyed puppydog enjoys ice cream more than we do," the Fuzzywump continued with a chuckle, "For, you know,

with his cross eyes he sees two dishes of ice cream instead of one, and it tastes just twice as good."

"Silly!" the puppydog replied, "You know better than that!"

"I know it!" the Fuzzywump agreed, "But really you should not look cross eyed."

"You see!" he explained to Raggedy Ann and Raggedy Andy, "The puppydog really isn't cross eyed. He does it because it makes him look funny."

"Let me see you straighten your eyes!" Raggedy Ann requested. And when the puppydog did this, Raggedy Ann and Andy both said, "You look ever so much cuter with your eyes straight."

"Then I shall not cross them again," the puppydog laughed.

"While you eat your ice cream, I shall tell you my story," the Fuzzywump suggested.

"When I was a little teeny weeny Fuzzywump boy, and went barefooted, I always got my feet dusty and dirty playing all day. So, every night when it was time to go to bed, my mother would say, 'Wumpie, you must wash your feet before you go to bed.' And, I would say, 'Alright mother!' and I wouldn't do it at all. Then in the morning mother would ask me if I had washed my neck and ears, and I would say, yes, and I had not done it."

"No wonder you grew so you couldn't say what you meant!" the puppydog said.

"Yes!" the Fuzzywump agreed, "One little fib is just like a seed. It grows and grows until, in the end you have a large clump of fib weeds. I had grown so in the habit of telling fibs, I couldn't tell the truth without meaning the opposite."

"I'll bet you missed a lot of fun!" Raggedy Ann said.

"Indeed I did!" the Fuzzywump agreed. "At last the fib weeds grew so high, I could not see my nice kind mother any more, so, I came here to live, all by myself, until the puppy-dog came to live with me."

"Now you won't tell any more fibs, will you?" the puppy-dog asked as he kissed the Fuzzywump. "Never!" the Fuzzywump replied.

"Perhaps, now that you have been turned right side up, you will be able to see your dear mother," Raggedy Andy said.

"I shall soon find out!" the Fuzzywump said as he ran and got his hat, "And you all can come with me!"

After the Fuzzywump had wrapped up his magic book, he locked the door and they all started out to find Fuzzywump's mother dear.

Chapter Two

HOW long has it been since you saw your dear mother?" Raggedy Ann asked the Fuzzywump as they walked along through the deep, deep woods.

"I haven't seen her since I was a little boy!" the Fuzzywump replied.

Raggedy Ann could not tell by this answer how long it had been, for, she could not tell whether the Fuzzywump was five, ten, fifteen, or fifty years old. But, anyway Raggedy Ann knew it must be a very long time, for, the Fuzzywump's eyes were filled with large tears and Raggedy Ann wiped them away with her little pocket hanky, the one with a little blue border on it.

When our friends had walked a long way through the woods, they stopped to rest by the side of the tumbling brooklet.

"Now if we could only find a nice soda water spring!" Raggedy Ann wished, "Or a field of cookies!"

"Now you have made me hungry!" the Fuzzywump cried

as he began untying the package which held his magic book. "Let's have something to eat!"

"Are you going to eat a story?" Raggedy Ann laughed.

"What a question!" Raggedy Andy exclaimed. "How can we eat a story, Raggedy Ann?"

"Well!" said the Fuzzywump, still untying the package, "We cannot eat a story!"

"Of course not!" Raggedy Andy agreed with a chuckle deep down in his cotton stuffed throat, "Of course not!"

"To be sure, we cannot eat a story!" the Fuzzywump went on, just as if the Raggedys had not interrupted him, "But, we can eat part of a story."

Raggedy Ann and Raggedy Andy laughed at this, but the little puppydog wagged his tail expectantly in front of the Fuzzywump.

"I never heard of anyone eating even a smidgin part of a story!" Raggedy Andy said, "Unless maybe billygoats do!"

"Maybe billygoats eat paper because there happens to be pictures or stories of pies and cakes and cookies printed on the paper!" Raggedy Ann suggested.

"Let's see!" the Fuzzywump mused, "What story shall we start with?"

"I do not care to eat part of any story!" Raggedy Ann said, very decidedly.

"BOW! WOW! WOW!" the puppydog barked, as he wiggle-waggled his tail and jumped up and down in front of the Fuzzywump.

"You must not talk dog talk!" the Fuzzywump laughed, as he patted the puppydog's head. "We cannot understand you!"

"I grew so anxious, I forgot what I was doing!" said the puppydog.

"Let's start with the witch's house in 'Hansel and Gretel.' It is made of gingerbread. The roof is of candy icing. The windows of thin transparent candy. The shutters are of chocolate cake. And the foundation is of rock candy."

Raggedy Ann and Andy did not see how anyone could eat part of a story, so they did not speak.

"We will start on the witch's house in the story of 'Hansel and Gretel' if you like," the Fuzzywump said as he

turned to the index.

"Page twenty-seven is the place!" the Fuzzywump mused as he turned the pages. "Ah! here we are!"

The Raggedys came close, and, looking in the book, they saw Hansel and Gretel walk through the forest until they came to the home of the witch. Then when Hansel and Gretel began eating pieces which they broke from the witch's house, the Fuzzywump and the puppydog jumped right in the book and began breaking pieces of gingerbread from the sides of the house.

"We were wrong about eating a part of a story!" the

Raggedys laughed as they, too, jumped into the book to join the others.

Raggedy Andy reached up to the roof and pulled off a very large piece of the candy icing. "RRRRRIPPP!" it sounded.

"Who is nibbling on my cunning little candy-gingerbread house?" a squeaky voice asked.

"We are!" Raggedy Ann answered.

The witch, a wrinkled old lady with a long nose came

thumping out of the house, and, catching the Fuzzywump, who happened to be standing nearest, dragged him inside and slammed the door.

Hansel and Gretel seemed surprised at the witch's action. "The story does not go that way, at all!" Gretel said. "The witch is supposed to catch Hansel and me."

"Perhaps we had better tell the witch!" Raggedy Ann suggested as she knocked softly on the candy door.

"Who is knocking at my candy door?" the witch asked from inside.

"You must come out and catch Gretel and me!" Hansel

cried. "You have someone who does not belong in the story."

"I know it, silly!" the witch called without opening the door. "I am tired of having the story go the same way all the time and having you and Gretel escape from me each time. So, now I shall make this fizzy-wizzy Fuzzywump into noodle soup as soon as he gets fat. You must all run along home and not bother me."

"We cannot leave the Fuzzywump!" Raggedy Ann said. "He will never find his mother if we do!"

Hansel and Gretel felt very sad for the Fuzzywump, and the puppydog sat down and held his nose up in the air and howled dismally.

Raggedy Ann sat down and pulled her rag forehead into a lot of wrinkles, for, that was the best way for her to think exceedingly hard.

Raggedy Andy sat and nibbled his piece of candy icing roof, and tried to think, but he could not think of any way to rescue the poor Fuzzywump.

Gretel told Raggedy Ann, "The witch always caught

Hansel and me and put us into a little coop. But the witch is so lazy, she took me out of the coop so that I could do the cooking for her. When the witch wanted Hansel to grow fat, she made me cook a lot of nice things for him. Then she would go to the coop and say, 'Hansel! stick out your little finger so that I may feel it to tell if you are getting fat.' And Hansel would stick out a thin little chicken bone. The witch, being very nearsighted, always thought it was Hansel's little finger."

"That was a good way to fool her!" Raggedy Andy laughed. "Maybe if I throw a candy stone through one of her windows the witch might become frightened and run out the back door. Then we could rescue the Fuzzywump from the coop before the witch knows what we have done."

"Oh, no!" Raggedy Ann exclaimed. "It is wrong to throw stones, even candy stones, through anyone's windows. Even those belonging to an old witch."

"Do you know whether there are any fine, wild soda water springs, or ice cream mud puddles around here?" Raggedy Andy asked Gretel.

"I do not believe there are any!" Gretel replied. "You see, Raggedy Andy, this story was written many years ago, and ice cream mud puddles had not been discovered then."

"That is too bad!" Raggedy Andy sighed, "For if Raggedy Ann could have an ice cream soda, I am sure she could think so much better, she would soon find a way to rescue the Fuzzywump from the witch's coop."

"What is that cunning little creature, there?" the witch asked as she opened her door and pointed to the puppydog.

“Why, that is the Fuzzywump’s puppydog!” Raggedy Ann explained.

“Come here, puppydog!” commanded the witch, and she whistled two or three times.

“The Fuzzywump wishes to speak to you!”

“What does he want?” the puppydog asked as he ran up on the witch’s candy porch.

The witch reached out a long arm and dragged the puppydog inside and slammed the door. “Ha, ha, ha!” she chuckled, “That’s the time I fooled you!”

“You told a big fib!” Raggedy Andy cried. “You should be ashamed of yourself!”

“Pooh! who cares?” the witch laughed through a crack in the candy door. “The puppydog is locked in the coop with the Fuzzywump and I will make noodle soup out of both of them, just like I always intended to do with Hansel and Gretel.”

“You’ll be sorry for this!” Raggedy Andy cried. “I’ll hunt up a policeman and have you arrested. That’s what! You’d better let the Fuzzywump and his puppydog out before I get the policeman!”

"I know you are trying to fool me, Raggedy Andy!" the witch squeaked. "There isn't a single policeman in this whole book, so, Mister Raggedy Andy, you cannot find one!"

"That is quite true!" Gretel whispered to Raggedy Andy. "We have never seen a single policeman. I'll walk around and peep in the kitchen window and see what the Fuzzywump is doing."

"Maybe you had better stay here, Gretel!" Raggedy Andy said. "I will go!" So, he walked around to the back of the witch's house.

Raggedy Andy stayed so long that Hansel walked around the house to see what was keeping him. "Raggedy Andy isn't there!" Hansel excitedly told Raggedy Ann and Gretel.

"Ha, ha, ha!" the witch chuckled. "Raggedy Andy is in the coop with the Fuzzywump and the puppydog."

"What shall we do?" Raggedy Ann asked Hansel and Gretel.

"You'd better run along home!" the witch cried. "For, if you do not mind your own business, I shall catch you and put you all in the coop."

"I shall take care that you do not catch me near your candy door!" Raggedy Ann told the witch.

Then Hansel and Gretel and Raggedy Ann walked away from the house of the witch and sat down where they could see the witch's candy door.

"We will soon find a way to rescue our friends!" Raggedy Ann promised.

"I am sorry that we opened the Fuzzywump's magical book to get something to eat!" Raggedy Ann sighed. "I wonder what our friends are doing?"

"I guess they are just sitting in the witch's coop," Hansel said, "That is what I used to do in every story."

SUN
WORTH GRUELLE

Yes, Raggedy Andy, the Fuzzywump and his puppydog were just sitting in the coop, waiting to be rescued.

"Here comes the witch!" Fuzzywump cried.

"Put your little fingers out so that I may tell if you are getting fat!" the witch whined.

"The Fuzzywump is the only one who has little fingers!" Raggedy Andy told the witch. "My hands are made of cloth and stuffed with cotton, and I only have thumbs on my hands." And, Raggedy Andy continued, "The puppydog hasn't any fingers because puppydogs only have toes."

"What had we better do?" the witch asked. "How can I tell if you are getting fat when I cannot feel your little fingers?"

"Maybe you could sew a little finger on Raggedy Andy's hand!" the puppydog suggested, with a sly wink at Raggedy Andy.

"I will get a needle and thread!" the witch cried, pleased with the idea. "Then I can make a little rag finger and sew it on Raggedy Andy's hand."

When the witch left the room, the puppydog whispered to the Fuzzywump and Raggedy Andy and the three giggled, just as if they were about to play a good joke on the witch. And, sure enough, when the witch returned and reached down into the coop and lifted Raggedy Andy out, Fuzzywump was hanging on to Raggedy Andy's legs and the puppydog was hanging on to the Fuzzywump's coat tails. But the witch, being nearsighted, did not know she was lifting all three out of the coop.

The Fuzzywump and his puppydog hid in back of the witch's chair while she sewed a little rag finger on Raggedy Andy's hand. Then, the witch put Raggedy Andy back in the coop and said, "Now, when I come back and ask if you are getting fat, you must stick your little rag finger out through a crack in the door so that I can feel it."

Raggedy Andy did not answer, for, he had to hold his hand over his mouth to keep from laughing out loud.

"I'll go put the water on to boil!" the witch remarked as she shuffled out of the room.

The Fuzzywump lifted Raggedy Andy out of the coop. "Let us hide under this large chair and see what the witch does when she finds out we are not in the coop!" the puppy-dog chuckled.

Presently the witch returned. "Stick your finger out, Raggedy Andy!" the witch commanded as she walked up to the coop and felt all about for Raggedy Andy's hand.

When the witch discovered there was no one in the coop, she sat down on the floor and began crying. "They have escaped!" she sobbed.

Raggedy Andy felt so sorry for the witch, he wiped the tears from her eyes with his new rag finger and the tears made it sopping wet. "I wanted to cook them!" the witch cried.

"We wouldn't be good if we were cooked!" Raggedy

Andy explained to the witch, "You might just as well cook your apron as cook me, for, I am made out of cloth like your apron. What you need to eat is an ice cream cone, or a lolly-pop, or a cream puff. They are really delicious."

"Then I wish I might have some!" the witch sighed, "For, I have never tasted any."

"The first time I find any, I shall see that you have some!" Raggedy Andy promised, as he kissed the witch goodbye.

"Thank you!" the witch said, as she opened the door and told Raggedy Andy, Fuzzywump, and the puppydog good-bye.

Chapter Three

"I AM very glad we escaped from the coop in the witch's candy house!" the Fuzzywump laughed as he and Raggedy Andy and the puppydog walked down the path.

"So am I!" Raggedy Andy agreed. "I wonder where Raggedy Ann and Hansel and Gretel are?"

"Maybe Raggedy Ann has climbed out of the magic book!" the Fuzzywump's puppydog suggested.

"How will we ever be able to get out of the magic book?" Raggedy Andy wanted to know.

The Fuzzywump stopped and thought. "Dear me!" he exclaimed, "I never thought of that. This is the first time I ever jumped into the magic book, so, I do not know how to get out again, unless someone finds the book and lifts us out."

The Fuzzywump sat down on a stone and cried into his pocket hanky. "Maybe I shall never see my nice mama

again, and we shall always have to live in the magic book."

"Do not cry!" said the puppydog as he kissed the Fuzzywump's hands. "It doesn't do any good to cry!"

"You are right!" the Fuzzywump agreed, brushing his eyes with the back of his hand and leaving a muddy streak across his face.

Raggedy Andy took the Fuzzywump's hanky and wiped the mud from his face. "I'll wash my hands in the first brook I come to!" the Fuzzywump said, "For if anyone has dirty hands, potatoes may start to grow on them."

Raggedy Andy asked the puppydog if he could track Raggedy Ann and Hansel and Gretel.

"Oh, yes!" the puppydog replied as he sniffed about. "I know they went this way, and they sat down here, and they went through these ferns, and,—there they are!"

The puppydog barked and ran to where Raggedy Ann sat talking to a funny little man.

"Oh! here's the Fuzzywump's cunning little puppydog, Mister Sinbad!" Raggedy Ann cried as she caught up the puppydog and hugged him as she was so glad to see him,

"And, here come the Fuzzywump and Raggedy Andy!"

"How did you escape from the witch's coop?" Sinbad the Sailor asked when Raggedy Ann had introduced him to the Fuzzywump and Raggedy Andy.

Raggedy Andy told how they had escaped and Sinbad laughed, "That was a good way to fool the witch!"

"I felt very sorry for her!" Raggedy Andy said. "Do you know, Mister Sinbad, the poor witch has never tasted an ice cream soda, a lolly-pop, or a cream puff?"

"Dear me! Is it possible?" Sinbad cried.

"I feel sorry for anyone who has never tasted them!" said Raggedy Ann.

"So do I!" Sinbad said as he took out his hanky and began crying.

"But you shouldn't cry, Mister Sinbad!" Raggedy Ann sympathized in her soft kindly cotton stuffed voice, "You will make your nose red!"

"Oh, dear! I can't help it!" Sinbad moaned. "I have never tasted any of those goodies either."

"No wonder you are crying!" Raggedy Ann said, "But, never mind, maybe we can find a place where cream puffs grow wild, beside a soda water fountain."

Sinbad wiped the tears from his eyes with Raggedy Ann's apron and said, "There is a queer little fountain right over there in the bushes. But the water is red and I was afraid to drink it."

Sinbad led the way and showed our friends the little red fountain which fizzed up in the air and then tinkled down into a large bowl. "Be careful that you do not step in the red mud all around the fountain!" Sinbad warned his friends.

There were little silver cups growing on short stems all about the fountain.

Raggedy Andy ran and picked one of the cups and filled it half full of the red "mud," then he dipped it in the fountain and handed it to Sinbad.

"Just you try this, Mister Sinbad!" Raggedy Andy smiled.

Then Raggedy Andy served the ice cream "mud" and red strawberry soda water to everyone, even the puppydog. And dashing away, he called, "I am going back and bring the witch. She will enjoy this, I am sure."

"Bring a large piece of her gingerbread house!" the Fuzzywump called after Raggedy Andy.

When Raggedy Andy returned with the witch, he found that Sinbad had enjoyed eleven ice cream sodas. The Fuzzywump ten and a half, Raggedy Ann four, and the puppydog two.

"Is this the witch who locked you up in her coop?" Sinbad asked when he was introduced to the witch.

"Yes!" Raggedy Andy answered, as he gave the witch an ice cream soda. "But, she really did not mean any harm. Did you, Mrs. Witch?"

"I do not believe I did!" the witch replied. "But anyway, I like you all very much now, and we shall be good friends."

"Indeed we shall!" Raggedy Ann laughed, "For it is such good fun being friends, and it never is fun at all disliking someone."

"The next time I catch Hansel and Gretel, I will not put them in the coop. Instead, I will bring them down here and give them sodas."

"These are the first ice cream sodas I have ever tasted!" Sinbad told the witch. "And they are very much better than I thought they would be."

"I don't see why we never discovered the ice cream mud

puddle and soda water fountain before," the witch said. "I wonder if Hansel and Gretel know it is here?"

"No!" Raggedy Ann told the witch, "Hansel and Gretel have never tasted sodas either."

"I have travelled all over the world, and I never even heard of ice cream sodas!" Sinbad exclaimed.

"That is strange, Mister Sinbad!" Raggedy Andy laughed. "Why, in every town in the United States you can find places where they serve ice cream sodas and they are called soda fountains."

"But, you forget, Raggedy Andy," explained Raggedy Ann, "Mister Sinbad and the witch are people in the stories which were written long, long before soda water was discovered."

Sinbad turned to the Fuzzywump's puppydog, "Will you please bite me on the leg?" he asked.

"Oh! I would not like to bite you, Mister Sinbad!" the puppydog exclaimed, "It is impolite!"

"I know it is!" Sinbad agreed, "But, I must be asleep, and if you bite me and I feel it, then I will know that I am awake."

"Please do not bite him very hard!" the witch said.

"I'll just bite him a little teeny weeny bite!" the puppy-dog promised.

"Ouch!" Sinbad cried, "I guess I am awake all right, but I would like to know how I can be eating ice cream sodas if they have not been discovered?"

Raggedy Ann laughed and said, "You see, Mister Sinbad, you and the witch are just people in stories, and the stories are in the Fuzzywump's magic book. So, when we grew hungry awhile ago, the Fuzzywump opened the magic book to the story of 'Hansel and Gretel.' When we saw Hansel and Gretel eating pieces of the witch's candy house, we all jumped into the magic book so we could eat some, too."

"And now, we do not know how to get out of the magic book!" the Fuzzywump cried.

"Why don't you stay in the magic book?" Sinbad asked, "We can have lots of fun, and we can all live together in the witch's magic candy house!"

"I would like to have time to sit around the fire each evening and tell you all of the wonderful adventures I had in my seven voyages to the many strange and interesting places all over the world."

"Thank you!" smiled the Fuzzywump, "But, you see, my dear friends, I must return home and see my nice mama, for, I have not seen her since I was a little boy."

"Oh! then you must go home right away!" the witch told the Fuzzywump, "Your mama must be worried about you!"

"Don't you know how to work magic, Missus Witch?" the Fuzzywump's puppydog asked, "Can't you magic us out of the magic book?"

"Dear me! I do not know the first thing about working

magic," the witch replied. "Whoever wrote the story about Hansel and Gretel just called me a witch, but did not write anything about me working magic."

"Isn't it too bad they didn't?" Raggedy Andy queried.

"I guess if they had, you would not have escaped from the witch's house!" Sinbad chuckled. "Maybe we can find a way to get you out of the magic book."

"Someone is nibbling on my candy house!" the witch cried. "I must run home at once!"

"Do not forget!" Raggedy Ann called after the witch, "If it is Hansel and Gretel, bring them here to enjoy the sodas with us!"

"I shall not forget!" the witch promised as she ran through the bushes toward her home.

"Let us hunt around and perhaps we may find a lollypop field!" Raggedy Andy suggested.

"Look at this queer flower bush!" Sinbad called after they had gone but a short distance.

"Don't you know what they are?" Raggedy Ann asked.

"I never saw anything like them before!" Sinbad replied.

Raggedy Ann picked a lot and passed them around. "They are lady finger cookies and are filled with raspberry jelly," she told Sinbad.

"And here are lots and lots of cream puffs growing in the grass, just like mushrooms!" the puppydog cried.

And, as the ice cream sodas had made them all very hungry, Raggedy Ann, Raggedy Andy, the Fuzzywump, Sinbad, and the puppydog sat in under the lady finger cookie bush and enjoyed themselves.

Sinbad entertained them with stories of his exciting adventures and danced his famous horn pipe, at which he had become quite expert from long years of practice.

“I hope the witch finds she has company and brings them here to enjoy the lady fingers and the cream puffs!” the puppydog said.

“It is nice for you to say that,” Raggedy Ann laughed as she patted the puppydog’s head, “For, whenever we are having a nice time, we can always add to our own happiness by sharing our pleasures with others.”

Chapter Four

I WISH I could stay and visit with you longer!" Sinbad said, "But, you know, I must go in search of adventure."

Raggedy Ann, Raggedy Andy, the Fuzzywump and his puppydog were very sorry to have Sinbad go. He was such a jolly, good natured fellow and had told them many strange stories as they sat beneath the lady finger bush.

Sinbad kissed Raggedy Ann goodbye and shook hands with Raggedy Andy and the Fuzzywump. "I wish I could take the cunning little puppydog with me!" he said.

The Fuzzywump laughed as he replied, "I wish that I had two puppydogs, Mister Sinbad, so that I could give you one. But, I love this puppydog so much, and he loves me so much, I know we would not be happy if we were separated."

"Oh! You must always keep the puppydog," Sinbad chuckled.

When Sinbad left them, the Fuzzywump said to Raggedy Ann, "Don't you think we should return to the witch's candy house? It was there we jumped into the magic book, and, I believe we must return there if we expect to get out of the magic book."

"The Fuzzywump is right!" the puppydog said. "We must return to the witch's candy house."

"We came from over in that direction, didn't we?" Raggedy Ann asked.

"I cannot remember!" the Fuzzywump replied.

And, do you know? Neither Raggedy Ann, Raggedy Andy, nor the puppydog could remember the way back to the candy house of the witch.

After a while our friends came to a tiny little path.

"It must have been made by a bunny!" the Fuzzywump said.

"If it was made by a bunny, he was wearing cunning little shoes," Raggedy Ann said. "See there are prints of cunning little, bitsie shoes in the dust."

Raggedy Ann, Raggedy Andy, the Fuzzywump and his puppydog followed the tiny path until they came to a lovely little house. The little house was not much larger than a dry goods box, but it had cunning little windows and doors and the roof was thatched.

"What a darling little house!" Raggedy Ann cried. "See how well kept the garden is, with the beautiful flowers growing everywhere."

As our good friends walked up to the house they heard someone inside weeping. "Who can be crying in such a lovely little house?" Raggedy Ann asked.

At the sound of Raggedy Ann's soft, kindly, cottony voice, the tiny front door opened and a cunning little dwarf with a long white beard came out.

"Why do you cry, so?" Raggedy Ann asked. "You have made your little nose as red as a ripe strawberry!"

"Oh! dear, Raggedy Ann!" the little dwarf replied, "You will cry, too, when I tell you what has happened."

"I live here with my six little dwarf brothers," the little dwarf said, "And we never have had anyone visit us until little Snow White came. We found her asleep in one of our tiny beds when we came home one evening. Just as soon as we saw her, we loved her. Little Snow White has lived with us ever since then."

"This morning my brothers and I went to the forest to work, and when we came home, I found dear little Snow White lying on the floor. And she cannot hear me when I speak to her."

"Dear me!" Raggedy Ann said, her candy heart filled with sympathy, "May we see her?"

The little dwarf led the way into the pretty little house, and there upon one of the tiny beds, lay beautiful little Snow White.

As Raggedy Ann and Raggedy Andy and the Fuzzy-wump and his puppydog stood looking at pretty Snow

WORTH
GRUELLE

White, the other six little dwarfs came in. When they saw Snow White lying so silent and still, they all began crying as if their tiny hearts would break.

"We shall never hear her singing and her happy laughter again!" they cried.

The Fuzzywump drew Raggedy Ann to one side and whispered, "I do not believe the seven dwarfs know they are living in the magic story book. And, as I have read the story many, many times, I know just what is the trouble with Snow White."

"She has a small piece of apple lodged in her throat and we must shake it out."

After they had whispered at length, Raggedy Ann called the seven little dwarfs into the kitchen. "You wait here for a moment and we will have lovely little Snow White laughing again!"

Then she and Raggedy Andy and the Fuzzywump went into the room where Snow White was lying, and, lifting her upside down, they shook the piece of apple from her throat.

Snow White laughed when she saw Raggedy Ann and Raggedy Andy. "What happy looking rag dolls!" she cried. "Did the seven little dwarfs bring you to me, as a present?"

The little dwarfs came running in when they heard Snow White laughing. And, they were all so happy to see Snow White alive again, they all wept for joy. So, Raggedy Ann had to wring the joy tears from her hanky, after she had wiped their eyes.

Raggedy Ann thought little Snow White far lovelier than the story book had told. And she knew her to be happy and kindly, as well as beautiful.

Little Snow White was a princess, but she enjoyed doing everything she could for the seven little dwarfs.

"I love to have dinner ready for them when they come home after working all day in the forest," Snow White told Raggedy Ann.

"I am sorry the mean old woman came today selling apples, for, from the moment I took a bite of the apple, I did not know another thing until I saw you standing there."

"She must have been a very mean old woman!" Raggedy Andy said.

"If we ever catch her about the place, we will make her jump!" one little dwarf cried as he shook his tiny fist.

"You bet we will!" the other six dwarfs chimed in.

"I'll help you get dinner!" Raggedy Ann told Snow White. "Where are the plates, the cups and saucers, and the knives and forks and spoons?"

Little Snow White laughed, and, catching Raggedy Ann's hands, danced Raggedy Ann out into the kitchen.

When little Snow White was out of the room, the Fuzzywump whispered to the little dwarfs, "Do you know who the old woman was that gave Snow White the apple?"

"No! We do not!" the seven dwarfs answered.

"Then I will tell you!" said the Fuzzywump. "The old woman is Snow White's stepmother. She put brown paint on her face and dressed in old clothes, so Snow White would not recognize her."

"Do you mean she was the queen?" the seven dwarfs asked in astonishment.

"Yes, indeed! That is just who she is!" the Fuzzywump replied. "You see, I have looked in this magic book many times, and have watched you go through the story of 'Snow White and the Seven Dwarfs.' "

"How can she be so mean to a lovely girl like Snow White?" Raggedy Andy asked.

"Well, I'll tell you!" the Fuzzywump replied, "The queen

is very beautiful herself, and it makes her peevish when her magic mirror tells her that Snow White is lovelier than she. So, the queen does all she can to keep Snow White from being lovelier."

"Dear me!" exclaimed Raggedy Andy, "I did not know anyone could be so selfish."

"Isn't it too bad?" the Fuzzywump said, "We should all be very happy for those who are more fortunate than we. For, if we let envy creep into our hearts, it makes us dissatisfied. And, when we grow discontented, we shut the doors of our hearts to the sunshine of happiness. So, you see, the queen has closed the door of her heart and is living

in the shadows of the wall her envy has built about her."

"Dinner is ready!" Raggedy Ann called into the room.

"Raggedy Ann is a wonderful help!" little Snow White told the dwarfs.

"You should see how she can knock the weenies off the frankfurter tree with a stick. It is much easier than shaking the tree."

Raggedy Ann, Raggedy Andy, the Fuzzywump and his puppydog all sat at the long table with Snow White and the seven dwarfs.

Snow White tied a napkin around the neck of the puppydog so that he would not spill anything in his lap, and then, one of the little dwarfs gave thanks for the dinner.

"I wish that I could throw sticks like Raggedy Ann!" Snow White said, "Why, she can knock four or five weenies from the tree every time she throws."

Raggedy Andy laughed happily at this, for he liked to have anyone praise Raggedy Ann.

"I wish we had a hot weenie tree growing in our yard!" the puppydog said.

"I have never seen a frankfurter tree before!" Raggedy Ann said. "The weenies steam all the time, Snow White tells me, and the weenies are always cooked."

"We planted a hot weenie out there years and years ago," one of the dwarfs remarked, "For, we knew, if it grew into a hot weenie tree, it would save us a lot of work when we came home from the forest in the evening. Sometimes we do not get home until late and it is nice to run out to the garden, pick a few wild buns, shake some hot weenies from the tree, and draw a pitcher of sparkling root beer from the root beer well."

"It makes housekeeping very easy!" Snow White laughed.

"When I came to live with my seven good friends, and saw the hot weenie tree, I suggested that they plant pan cakes, and boiled eggs, and everything like that. Well, the dwarfs did, and now we have the most wonderful garden you have ever seen, or could wish for. After dinner, I will

take you out so you may see it. I never pick the ice cream cones until we are ready for dessert, for they melt too rapidly."

"We wish we did not have to go to the forest to work today," the dwarfs said, "We would all have a fine picnic over by the river."

"That would be lovely!" Raggedy Ann told the dwarfs, "But, it would not be right for you to neglect your work just to give us a nice time. We will stay and play with Snow White!"

"We will be very glad if you will stay and play with Snow White!" one of the dwarfs said, "For, we are afraid she must grow lonesome at times!"

Snow White kissed all of the little dwarfs goodbye and told Raggedy Ann, "Really, I never get lonesome, for the dear little dwarfs have made so many lovely things for me to play with, I couldn't grow lonesome if I tried. Just you come out and see the fine swing the dwarfs made for me. It runs by clockwork and you never need anyone to push you to swing as high as you wish. And there is the whirling jinney with seats on it so you may sit and ride and ride as long as you care to. I always pretend I am at an amusement park. And, I have tickets and pretend the ticket man comes to collect them for each ride. My goodness! We need never grow lonesome when we can amuse ourselves by pretending someone is playing with us."

"I know what let's do!" the Fuzzywump cried, "Let's play on the whirling jinney, or merry-go-round. I'll be the ticket man, Raggedy Ann can be the mama, Raggedy Andy can be the daddy, and Snow White can be the little girl."

"That will be fun!" Snow White laughed. "Let's start right in!"

"Hadn't we better do the dishes first?" asked practical Raggedy Ann. "You know," she explained to Snow White, "After we have played awhile, it won't be as much fun to stop and do the dishes. It is better to do our work first, then we will have all the rest of the time for play."

Snow White caught Raggedy Ann and tossed her up in the air and caught her as she came down. "How true that is, Raggedy Ann. If there were any dishes to wash and wipe, I would do them before I start to play. But these dishes, after we have left the table, roll out to the kitchen, fly up into the sink and wash themselves. Then they wipe themselves dry with the dish towel and carefully place themselves in the cupboard."

"Are they magic dishes?" Raggedy Ann wished to know.

"I do not believe so!" Snow White replied, "The dwarfs had them when I first came here to live. They told me they got the dishes when they were quite small and trained them to wash and wipe themselves and place themselves on the cupboard shelves."

"It must have taken a great amount of patience to teach the dishes," Raggedy Ann laughed.

"Indeed! I guess it did!" Snow White said. "At first the dishes had the bad habit of dropping themselves on the floor and breaking."

"I wonder why that was?" the Fuzzywump asked.

"I suppose because dishes have grown accustomed to being dropped so much by careless people, it is just a habit they have. But, the little dwarfs soon broke the dishes of that habit," laughed Snow White. "And, I believe anybody can train their dishes not to drop, if they hold the dishes very carefully when they are being washed and wiped.

Now, let's play on the whirling jinney!"

The whirling jinney which the dwarfs had made for Snow White was painted white with gold trimmings. The seats were fitted with soft cushions of crimson velvet and a large music box played sweet music as the jinney whirled 'round and 'round.

Raggedy Ann, Raggedy Andy, and the Fuzzywump enjoyed riding on the whirling jinney with Snow White. But the puppydog said it made him feel as though his eyes really were crossed, so, he hopped off and ran and barked at the frankfurter tree until a hot weenie fell off.

While he was eating the frankfurter, the puppydog heard someone knocking at the front door. He ran around the house and saw an old woman standing there.

"BOW! WOW! WOW!" the puppydog barked.

The old woman raised her stick. "You go away!" she shouted. "I looked in my magic looking-glass and found out that Snow White is still more beautiful than I, so, I have come to comb her hair so she will fall down on the floor as she always does in the story."

"Aha!" the puppydog exclaimed. "You are the mean old stepmother queen in disguise!" And he jumped about the queen and clicked his teeth so near her ankles, she dropped her basket and stick and went running for home as fast as she could go.

The puppydog chased the queen far into the woods, then

he came back and buried the comb the queen had intended for Snow White.

The puppydog then smiled to himself as if to say, "I have a secret." And wagging his tail happily, he went around the house and barked at the frankfurter tree until three weenies grew excited and fell off.

Chapter Five

ONE nice thing about the whirling jinney in the back yard of the home of the seven little dwarfs was that the whirling jinney went 'round and 'round without anything making it go. And it never wore out.

Snow White would say, "Whirl around, jinney!" when she wanted it to go, and "Stop, jinney!" when she wished it to stop.

It was a lot of fun. For, a whirling jinney cannot be found in every back yard.

While Raggedy Ann, and Raggedy Andy, and the Fuzzywump rode on the whirling jinney with Snow White, the puppydog had lots of fun barking at the frankfurter tree and eating the weenies as they fell off. And, because the puppydog had been barking so much, none of our friends paid any attention when he ran around the house barking as loudly as he could. The puppydog had heard the front gate squeak and he knew someone was coming. "If it is the mean queen, I'll nip her heels this time to teach her a lesson," the puppydog thought.

The front gate had almost stopped squeaking when the

puppydog came bouncing around the house. He saw a little old woman coming down the path. "BOW! WOW! WOW!" the puppydog barked, forgetting in his excitement he could talk as well as anyone. Then he yelled in puppydog language, "I'll nip your heels!"

The strange little old woman came straight on and never paid the least attention to the puppydog even when he nipped her heels. This surprised the puppydog very much, for he had never yet met anyone who did not care when they

had their heels nipped. So, the puppydog sat down and scratched behind his ear with his front left foot, and tried to think.

The little old woman knocked at the front door with her stick—"CRACK! CRACK! CRACK!"

"It isn't the queen!" the puppydog said out loud.

"Were you speaking to me?" the little old woman asked.

"I said that you are not the mean old queen!" the puppydog replied. "I am sorry that I nipped your heels!"

"I didn't know you nipped my heels," the little old woman chuckled. "I heard you barking at me when I came down the front walk and I knew that barking dogs never bite."

This puzzled the puppydog, so he sneezed to cover his embarrassment.

"Where is everybody?" the little old woman asked.

"The dwarfs have gone to the forest to work. Raggedy Ann, Raggedy Andy, and the Fuzzywump are playing with Snow White on the whirling jinney," advised the puppydog.

"Oh, how nice!" the little old woman laughed. "I am

glad Snow White has nice company."

When the puppydog and the little old woman walked around the house, the puppydog said, "Will you please knock down a few of the weenies from the frankfurter tree?"

So the agreeable old woman threw her stick up in the tree and eight weenies were so surprised they came tumbling down. "Thank you!" the puppydog said.

"Here's Granny!" Snow White cried when she spied the little old woman. She stopped the jinney and ran and threw her arms about the little old woman.

Snow White's Granny was happy to meet Raggedy Ann, and Raggedy Andy, and the Fuzzywump.

"I knew the queen was coming over, so I hurried to get here to tell you."

"I chased the queen away just a few minutes ago!" the puppydog laughed.

"Possibly then, she will not return!" Granny said. "So, I will take off my things."

"How is the dress bush, and the stocking vine, and the shoe tree this morning?" she asked Snow White.

"They are just loaded with pretty things," Snow White replied as she opened a gate and they all walked back into another garden.

Snow White and Raggedy Ann helped Granny select a beautiful dress from the dress bush, stockings from the stocking vine, and shoes from the shoe tree—and all matched perfectly.

Raggedy Ann, and Raggedy Andy, and the Fuzzywump and his puppydog were greatly surprised when the little old woman combed her hair and changed to her lovely new clothes, to see how pretty she was.

"Maybe I had better make some doughnuts before we start playing again!" Granny said with a sly wink at Raggedy Andy.

So, everybody went into the kitchen with Granny while she made the nicest doughnuts they had ever tasted—all covered with powdered sugar and with the nicest round holes. And they all ate the doughnuts as fast as Granny made them.

"I wonder why the queen tries to harm Snow White?" Raggedy Andy wished to know. "Everyone should be pleased because Snow White is so beautiful."

"Yes, indeed they should!" Granny agreed, "But the queen is different from most people. So, while these doughnuts cook, I will tell you why she is different."

"When the queen was a little girl about the size of Snow White, she was given everything she asked for. If she wanted a new doll every day of the week, she got a new doll each day. No matter what she wished for, it was given to her. So, you see, she had so many things, she did not prize any of them as she should. She grew so discontented with everything that she got in the habit of pouting and crying and frowning. Then, the first thing she knew, her face

which had been so pretty, was the face of a crosspatch."

"Dear me, how sad!" Raggedy Ann mused.

"Yes, indeed!" agreed Granny, "You know how it is, when children are not happy inside their unhappiness soon shows on the outside, and then people do not care to have them around. Soon, this was what happened to this little girl and it made her mother and daddy unhappy to see their little girl growing so ugly.

One day the little girl's daddy visited a great wizard. The wizard gave him a magic powder and a magic looking-glass which always told the truth.

When the little princess' daddy returned home, he told the princess to look in the magic glass and see who was ugly. And when she did, the magic glass said, 'You are the ugly one!' Then the daddy put the magic powder on his daughter's face and told her to ask the looking-glass who was the prettiest. So, the little princess asked the magic glass, 'Mirror, mirror, on the wall, who is the fairest one of all?' And the magic glass replied, 'You are the fairest one of all!'

So, Granny continued, the little princess grew up to be a very beautiful woman, and, when Snow White's mama went away to Fairyland, the princess became Snow White's stepmother, the queen.

One day the queen asked the magic glass who was the prettiest of all, and the looking-glass told her that Snow White was the loveliest of all. That is why the queen wishes to harm Snow White."

Granny then held up her finger, "Shh!" she said, "I just heard the front door squeak. Let us all remain quiet, and have Snow White go to the door. If it is the queen, ask her into the house."

Everyone was very quiet. And, sure enough, it was the queen disguised as an old apple woman.

"I have brought you some lovely apples!" the queen said to Snow White.

"Thank you! I do not care for any!" Snow White replied politely.

"They are lovely!" the queen said. "See! here is a red and green one. I will eat the green part and you may have the nice red part." And with this the queen started eating the green part of the apple.

Just then, Raggedy Ann and Raggedy Andy and the Fuzzywump ran into the room crying, "Do not eat any part of the apple, Snow White! It is the mean queen!"

The queen was so excited she forgot what she was doing, and took a bite of the red part of the apple. As soon as she did, she fell to the floor.

Raggedy Ann and the others crowded around the queen. The Fuzzywump was the first to speak, "Let us wash the brown paint from the queen's face and see how pretty she is!" So, Raggedy Ann washed the queen's face and they found the queen to be very beautiful.

Raggedy Ann, who has a candy heart with the words "I LOVE YOU" printed upon it, felt very sorry for the queen.

"Let us shake the piece of apple from her throat, just as we did with Snow White!" Raggedy Ann suggested.

They all thought this a splendid idea and went right to work on the queen. The piece of apple was soon shaken from the queen's throat and Raggedy Ann said, "Now I will work some magic and make the queen happy, even though Snow White is lovelier."

Raggedy Ann borrowed the little crooked stick which the Fuzzywump had given Raggedy Andy, and tapped the queen upon the head. "Hokus! Pokus!" Raggedy Ann cried, three times. "Now you will be happy!"

Immediately everybody was happy, for, they saw a lovely smile appear on the face of the queen as the queen hugged Snow White.

"I shall never be mean to you again, lovely Snow White!" the queen promised.

Raggedy Ann ran out into the garden and picked a lovely dress from the dress bush. The puppydog ran out and barked at the hot weenie tree and six frankfurters fell off.

When the queen put on the lovely dress Raggedy Ann had brought her, she was indeed, very beautiful.

So, Granny, knowing how the excitement must have made everyone very hungry, said, "Let us gather everything nice from the garden and have a wonderful surprise party for the seven little dwarfs. It is almost time for them to return from their work in the forest."

When the seven cunning little dwarfs came in they were so happy to find that Snow White's stepmother had changed from a mean queen to one who was as happy and friendly as dear old Granny.

"Have you noticed?" Raggedy Ann whispered to

Granny, "The queen is getting prettier every minute, and, it is because she has grown prettier inside."

Snow White's Granny laughed a soft Granny laugh and replied, "What you say is very true, Raggedy Ann. If the queen had but known that when she was a little girl, she would have had this much happiness all of her life. For, every hour can be made sunny if we only have our hearts filled with unselfish, kindly thoughts toward others."

When everyone, even the puppydog, had eaten as many cream puffs, ice cream cones, and other goodies as he wished, the queen said, "Now that Snow White and I are such good friends, I hope she will return with me and live in the castle."

Snow White kissed the queen and said, "Thank you very much, but what would the seven cunning little dwarfs do without me?" There would be no one to greet them when they returned from their work in the forest. I believe I shall live here and come over to see you whenever you wish me to come."

"I do not blame you," the queen laughed. "And I know just how the little dwarfs would miss you. So, you stay here where you have the whirling jinney and all the other wonderful things. Every day I will send the royal coach over to bring you to visit me at the castle."

"Isn't it nice?" Raggedy Andy whispered to the Fuzzywump, "Everything turned out happily, just like in a fairy tale book."

"Ha, ha, ha, Raggedy Andy!" the Fuzzywump laughed. "Don't you remember? It is a fairy tale and we are in the stories in my magic book."

"Everything was so real, I had forgotten!" Raggedy Andy replied. "And now, we must try to find our way out of the magic book so you may return to your dear mother."

Chapter Six

"WHAT I would like to know!" Raggedy Ann said as she and Raggedy Andy and the Fuzzywump and his puppydog walked away from the house of the seven dwarfs, "Is, how I worked the magic which changed the queen from such a mean queen into a nice happy queen?"

"It may have been because we washed her face," the Fuzzywump suggested.

"Perhaps Snow White worked the magic," the puppydog thought.

"But Snow White did not say anything, nor did she come near while I worked the magic to change the queen. Remember, I took the little crooked stick out of Raggedy Andy's pocket and tapped the queen's head with it," Raggedy Ann reminded them.

"Maybe it is a magic stick!" Raggedy Andy suggested.

"Was the little crooked stick which you gave Raggedy

Andy, a magic stick?" Raggedy Ann asked the Fuzzywump.

"Really, I do not know!" the Fuzzywump replied. "I just wanted to give Raggedy Andy something, so I took the little stick from the mantel and gave it to him."

"Where did you get the stick?" Raggedy Ann asked the Fuzzywump.

"Well!" began the Fuzzywump, "One day I was walking through the woods and I came to a funny little house built upon the top of a high stump and there was a ladder running up to the funny little house.

As I walked along, I heard someone call to me and ask—'Do you want to rescue a fairy princess who is shut up in this funny little house?' I looked up. And there was a funny little man looking out of a funny little window.

You will recall that at that time, I said just the opposite of what I really meant. So, I said, 'No! I do not wish to rescue the fairy princess.' 'Then you may come up the ladder!' the funny little man told me. I climbed the ladder and went into the house.

The funny little man asked me if I liked fairy princesses. And, although I meant the opposite, I replied, 'No, I do not like them at all.'

'That is good!' the funny man chuckled, 'For I have a very pretty little fairy princess shut up in that closet and I shall sell her to the first circus man that comes along!'

'That is a good idea!' I told the man. But really meant that I did not think it was.

'I like you for shutting the pretty little fairy princess in the closet.'

'I am very glad to hear you say so!' he said, 'For I have to go to a meeting of magic workers tonight and I want someone to stay here and see that the fairy princess does not escape while I am away. Would you like to stay?'

'I will see that she does not escape,' I told him. But, of course, I meant I would do my best to rescue the princess.

'I will give you six pennies to watch her for me,' the funny man said.

'Give me the pennies!' I cried, but meaning, 'I do not want your pennies.'

So, he gave me the pennies, put on his coat, and climbed down the ladder.

I sat and read a book for a long, long time to be sure he had gone far enough. Then I unlocked the closet, and there was the prettiest, the loveliest, the dearest, little fairy

princess you could imagine.

'I am sorry I unlocked the closet door so you might escape!' I told the princess.

She laughed a little tinkly laugh. Just like the merry sound of a tiny silver bell. Then she went to a box behind one of the doors and picked up the stick which I gave to Raggedy Andy.

'Here!' the fairy princess said to me, 'Is something which Wizzy Wizzard (that is the funny little man's name) took away from me, and you may have it.'

'I would love to have the stick!' I told the princess, meaning that I did not care for it at all.

This seemed to please her very much, so I took the stick."

"What a wonderful adventure!" Raggedy Ann said, "The fairy princess really escaped from Wizzy Wizzard?"

"Oh, yes!" exclaimed the Fuzzywump. "She thanked me and flew away. So, then I climbed down the ladder and went home. Soon after that you and Raggedy Andy came along, and I gave Raggedy Andy the stick."

"But," Raggedy Andy said, "It should belong to you. It may be a very magical stick."

"Oh, no!" the Fuzzywump laughed, "I believe it is just an ordinary little crooked stick. And anyway I do not want it, so it is yours."

After walking through the forest in the magical book for a long, long way, Raggedy Ann and Raggedy Andy and the Fuzzywump and his puppydog came to a house.

Raggedy Ann knocked softly on the door with her rag hand but no one answered. "I guess no one is at home!" Raggedy Ann said to the others who stood right behind her.

Just then the door flew open and a bear, a great big bear, ran out, so fast he knocked Raggedy Ann, Raggedy Andy, and the Fuzzywump head over heels and sent them rolling in the grass but they did not stay there very long.

This did not hurt Raggedy Ann nor her friends at all, nor did it hurt the puppydog who jumped up real quickly and nipped the big old bear just above the top of his slipper.

"Ouch!" the bear cried. Then seeing the puppydog, the bear asked, "Was it you who nipped me on the ankle, puppy-dog?"

"Yes sir!" the puppydog replied very politely. For he saw that his friends were not hurt and, besides, the bear was so very large.

"HMM!" said the big, large bear, "I'll bet a nickel you tore a hole in my stocking. I'll just bet!"

By this time two more bears had come out of the house and stood looking on. One was a medium sized mama bear and the other was a teeny weeny baby bear.

"I am sorry, Mister Bear!" the puppydog said. "You came out of the door so fast and upset my friends and I nipped your heel before I stopped to think."

"Well, anyway it did not hurt and since you did not tear

a hole in my stocking, everything is all right. I do not like to have holes in my stockings. Do you?" he asked Raggedy Ann.

"I certainly do not!" Raggedy Ann replied.

It was the largest bear Raggedy Ann had ever seen. And, although this bear seemed to be a very nice bear, still Raggedy Ann was a bit excited.

"Did she get away again?" mama bear asked the big, large bear.

"She always does, you know!" the daddy bear replied.

At this the baby bear began to cry like a little squeaky Teddy bear.

"Does he have a pain?" the Fuzzywump's puppydog asked.

Mama bear threw back her head and laughed until the flowers almost wiggled off her bonnet. "Land sakes! no!" she said. "He always wants us to catch Goldilocks. And that was who daddy bear was after when he upset you."

"I am sorry if I seemed rude!" apologized daddy bear. "But, really I did not know you were standing right in front of the door."

"Goldilocks did not come out of the house while we were here," the Fuzzywump said, "Or we would have seen her."

"She always jumps out of the upstairs window," mama bear explained.

"Will you come in? We were just out for a walk while our porridge cooled."

Raggedy Ann, Raggedy Andy, the Fuzzywump, and the puppydog followed the three bears into the cunning bear home. It was such a cozy home with a nice fireplace and very comfy chairs; one large one for the daddy bear, a middle sized chair for the mama bear, and a little teeny baby chair for the baby bear.

Mama bear put on plates for their new friends and daddy bear pulled up chairs for everyone, even the puppy-dog. For, of course, he was hungry too.

"Goldilocks only eats the porridge," mama bear laughed, as she passed a large plate of cream puffs to Raggedy Ann. "If she would only visit us sometime when we are at home, we would soon show her how friendly we can be."

"If we see her, we will tell her that you would like to have her for supper sometime," the Fuzzywump said.

Daddy bear laughed in a great big bear voice, "HAW! HAW! HAW!—only much louder. Mama bear laughed in a middle sized bear's voice, "HA! HA! HA!" And the baby bear laughed in his teeny weeny baby bear voice, "He! He! He!"

Then daddy bear chuckled, "Please do not tell Goldilocks that we would like to have her for supper. Tell her we would like to be friends with her and would like to have her eat supper with us."

After they had eaten all the cream puffs and all the tapioca pudding with cream on it, and a large bowl of cookies, daddy bear took off his shoes and put on his house slippers. Baby bear ran and brought daddy bear's long pipe. Everyone pulled chairs up to the fireplace and daddy bear told stories until it was time to go to bed.

"You must stay all night with us!" he invited, as he wound the clock. "Baby bear can sleep with mama bear and, as you are all quite small, you may all sleep together on baby bear's bed."

Mama bear led the way upstairs with a candle, and, when everyone was settled comfortably in bed, daddy bear blew out the candle. Raggedy Ann and her friends were lying in the nice pleasant dark, which, when the light goes

out, seems to cover one just like a soft kindly blanket. And so, with pleasant thoughts running through their heads, they were all soon fast asleep.

In the morning mama bear called upstairs to the others, "Time for everyone to get up!"

Daddy bear had been up a long time.

Raggedy Ann and Raggedy Andy rubbed the sleepy dust from their shoe button eyes and helped baby bear to dress. Then they all ran down stairs and washed their hands and faces in the cool spring water at the kitchen door.

"While the breakfast porridge cools, we'll take a walk in the woods. There is nothing that gives you such an appetite as a nice brisk walk before breakfast," mama bear said. "When we return we will have some nice pan cakes and maple syrup."

"Maybe Goldilocks will visit us while we are away," the baby bear thought.

"Then I will stay here and watch for her," Raggedy Ann laughed. "My appetite is always good because I am stuffed with nice clean white cotton. So, if Goldilocks comes I will tell her how nice you are and perhaps she will stay."

"That will be nice!" mama and daddy bear both agreed.

And, sure enough, the bears, Raggedy Andy, the Fuzzy-wump and his puppydog had hardly reached the bend in the path when Goldilocks came across the garden and knocked at the door.

"Come in!" Raggedy Ann called in her cheeriest voice.

Goldilocks hesitated, but then she thought, "That does not sound like a bear's voice." So, she opened the door and walked into the kitchen.

Wasn't she surprised to see Raggedy Ann there? "A nice rag doll!" Goldilocks laughed.

"I am Raggedy Ann!" Raggedy Ann introduced herself.

"And you can talk, too!" Goldilocks cried. "Do you belong to baby bear?"

Then Raggedy Ann told Goldilocks all about the three bears.

"They were in hopes you would come, Goldilocks! That is why I stayed here, so that I might ask you to stay for breakfast!"

"Will the three bears bite?" Goldilocks asked.

"Dear me, no!" Raggedy Ann told Goldilocks. "They are the nicest kindliest bears you ever saw."

"Then I will stay!" Goldilocks agreed, "For I am very, very hungry!"

The three bears were delighted when they returned to find Goldilocks visiting with Raggedy Ann.

Mama bear served everyone with porridge and cream. Then she baked twenty-leven golden pan cakes, light and fluffy which she served with maple syrup.

"Does your mama bake pancakes?" Raggedy Ann asked Goldilocks when she saw the little girl had eaten nine pancakes and liked them very much.

"Dear me, I haven't any mama!" Goldilocks brushed a tear from her eye. "I live all alone in a large hollow tree and never eat anything but berries and nuts, unless I come here when the bears are not at home and eat their porridge."

Mama, daddy, and baby bear all had tears in their eyes when Goldilocks told them this. For, they were very, very tender hearted bears.

"Then you must stay and live here with us," mama bear said. "We shall not let you live in an old hollow tree any longer."

"Indeed, we will not!" daddy bear cried in his deep, gruff voice.

And, as Goldilocks liked the kindly bears, she told them she would be very happy to live with them and help mama bear cook and keep house.

Mama bear filled a great basket with cream puffs, lady finger cakes, sandwiches, jelly doughnuts, and cookies. "We will celebrate with a picnic down by the river and have a very pleasant day," she laughed.

Then, with their hearts beating with happiness, the three bears, Goldilocks, Raggedy Ann, Raggedy Andy, the Fuzzywump and his puppydog all started for the winding river through the deep, deep woods.

Chapter Seven

WHEN Raggedy Ann, Raggedy Andy, the three bears, Goldilocks, the Fuzzywump and his puppy-dog came to the river where the grass was just as soft as a silken rug, they all sat down while mama bear passed around lady finger cakes, cream puffs, dill pickles, and all the other goodies.

"You have never told us where you came from," mama bear said to Raggedy Ann. "Nor where you and the Fuzzy-wump are going."

"The Fuzzywump is on his way to see his nice mother," Raggedy Ann explained. "But, you see, the Fuzzywump has a very magical book. We jumped into the magic book to nibble some of the candy icing from the house of the witch in the story of 'Hansel and Gretel.' Now we cannot find our way out of the book."

"Perhaps mama bear and I can help you," daddy bear suggested.

"Here comes someone!" Raggedy Andy whispered, "Maybe they can tell us which way to go to get out of the Fuzzywump's magic book."

Through the bushes, Raggedy Ann saw a pretty little girl with a red cape and hood walking toward them. And in her hand she carried a little basket. As everyone peeped through the bushes, they saw a great, large wolf run up to the little girl. "Can I help you carry your basket, Little Red Riding Hood?" the wolf asked.

"Oh, no thank you!" Little Red Riding Hood answered. "It is not heavy, and grandmother lives just behind those trees. I am going to spend the day with her. She is ill and cannot come to my house."

"I am sure you will have a nice time with your grandmother," the wolf laughed. Then he asked, "Won't you climb upon my back and let me carry you?"

"Thank you, Mister Wolf!" Little Red Riding Hood replied. "I wish to pick some wild flowers for grandma, but, you may walk along with me if you care to."

"Were you trying to carry off this little girl?" the

Fuzzywump's puppydog asked as he sniffed around the heels of the wolf.

"Please do not nip my heels," the wolf requested of the puppydog. "I am very fond of children and I usually carry Little Red Riding Hood on my back to the home of her nice grandmother."

"Then I will not nip your heels!" the puppydog promised.

"We were just having a picnic, Mister Wolf!" daddy bear said, "Won't you and Red Riding Hood join us? We have lady fingers, cream puffs, and all sorts of good things."

The wolf patted the puppydog on the head and sat down

on the soft grass beside Little Red Riding Hood. "I would like a cream puff, if you have one to spare," he laughed.

"I would like a cream puff to take to grandmother," Little Red Riding Hood told daddy bear.

"You wait here, Little Red Riding Hood," the wolf whispered, "I'll run to Granny's house and bring her here!" And away he trotted through the woods.

"Now is the time for me to try Raggedy Andy's little crooked stick," said Raggedy Ann. "I will find out if it is really and truly a magical stick."

Raggedy Ann wiggled the little crooked stick around and wished that Little Red Riding Hood's grandmother would not be ill. And, sure enough, in a jiffy the kindly

WORTH
GRUELLE

wolf came running up, pulling a little wagon with red wheels. Granny was sitting in the wagon laughing and she wasn't ill at all.

"Now we can have a fine picnic," the wolf laughed, "For over behind those large stones, there is one of the finest soda water springs you ever saw. And right beside it is a lovely ice cream mud puddle surrounded by candy covered cookie and lollypop bushes."

So the wolf led the way to the soda water spring and with the sandwiches, cream puffs, and other goodies in mama bear's basket, you can imagine what a lovely picnic it was.

"Do you know, Mister Wolf!" Raggedy Ann laughed when she saw the wolf help everyone to cream puffs, ice cream soda water, dill pickles, and everything else before he helped himself, "I thought maybe you were a naughty, mean old bad wolf when I saw you run up to Little Red Riding Hood."

"Dear me!" the wolf laughed in reply, "I am glad you do not think so now, Raggedy Ann!"

"So am I!" Raggedy Ann said, "But in the story of Little Red Riding Hood, you were not a nice gentlemanly wolf at all!"

"The wolf slapped his knee and chuckled, "Whoever told that story about me was mistaken. For, I always try to do for others just what I would like them to do for me. So, perhaps it was some other wolf."

"No! It must have been you!" Raggedy Ann replied, "Because you are in the story of 'Little Red Riding Hood' just like the three bears are in the story of 'Goldilocks.' "

"And were they wicked in the story?" the wolf asked as he filled Raggedy Ann's dish with chocolate ice cream from the ice cream mud puddle.

"They were not exactly wicked," Raggedy Ann replied. "But they did chase Goldilocks!"

"There, you see!" the wolf laughed as he gave daddy bear a pat on the shoulder, "Someone must have turned the stories inside out!"

"Perhaps someone did! Can you tell us how the story really should be told?" Raggedy Ann asked.

"We will let Little Red Riding Hood tell it while I get you all some lollypops," the wolf said.

"Whenever I went to visit grandmother, mother always said to me, 'Now watch out when you go through the woods that the Grung does not try to take the goodies from your basket,' " Little Red Riding Hood began.

"Whatever can a Grung be?" the Fuzzywump wanted to know. "I am sure I have never seen one."

"Oh, the Grung is a great big creature!" Little Red Riding Hood replied. "He is very fond of cakes and cookies. He has four legs and a long tail and is a very comical animal. So, when I walked through the woods, the very first day, the Grung came up to me and said, 'I'll bet a nickel your basket is filled with just the kind of goodies I like." 'Yes sir, Mr. Grung!' I replied, 'The basket is filled with goodies that I am taking to my grandmother, who is ill.'

'Then I must eat the goodies!' the Grung cried as he reached for my basket.

And, I am sure the Grung would have eaten Granny's goodies if the wolf had not stepped between us and cried, 'Now, Mister Grung, you run home to your mama and leave Little Red Riding Hood in peace!'

'Ha, ha, ha, who is afraid of you?' the Grung cried, very rudely.

And, he made his ears stick up straight just as he always does when he wants to fight and does not wish to step

WORTH
GRUELLE

on them. Of course, when the Grung did this, the wolf boxed the Grung's ears on both sides of his head so hard, the Grung's head must have rung like a door bell. Then, the wolf tied six knots in the Grung's long tail and took me to Granny's house."

"And did the Grung ever bother you after that?" Raggedy Ann wanted to know.

"Indeed, he did not!" Little Red Riding Hood replied with a laugh. "Mister Wolf taught him a lesson that first day."

"Dear me!" Raggedy Ann cried as she pointed through the woods, "Can that be the Grung coming along the path?"

A great big funny looking creature was coming toward our friends.

"Yes, it is the Grung!" the wolf told them. "But do not be alarmed. I shall not let him harm anyone!"

"Pooh!" Raggedy Andy exclaimed. "Nobody is afraid of the Grung. I can wrestle him so hard he will be sorry he ever bothered us." And brave little Raggedy Andy rolled up his sleeves.

Raggedy Andy stepped right out in front of the Grung when he walked up near our friends. Raggedy Andy challenged, "Do you want to wrestle, Mr. Grung?"

"Please do not wrestle me, Raggedy Andy!" the Grung pleaded. And everyone could see that the Grung's nose was red from weeping.

Raggedy Andy felt so sorry for the Grung, he borrowed Raggedy Ann's pocket hanky and wiped the tears from the Grung's eyes. "Now do not cry any more!" Raggedy Andy told the Grung. "Only cry babies cry. And a great big large Grung like you should not cry."

"Maybe a bee has stung him!" the puppydog said. "I was stung by a bee once and I had to hop along on three feet and carry the other one and it hurt very much."

"No, that is not the reason he is crying!" the Fuzzy-wump said, "For, he is walking on four feet."

"Maybe the bee sat down on top of the Grung's head!" the puppydog sighed, "It burns. For a bee's feet are very hot when she sits down!"

"No, I haven't been stung by a bee!" the Grung sobbed. "I am sobbing because I cannot untie the last knot Mister Wolf tied in my tail. I am afraid if I start to jump from

the top of one tree to the top of another, my tail will get caught, and I will just hang there and never be rescued."

Raggedy Andy hastened to untie the knot in the Grung's tail and then asked, "How can you jump from the top of one tree to another? You are so heavy you would break the branches!"

"Oh, I can't jump from one tree top to another," the Grung replied, "But I have always wanted to!"

"There, you see how unnecessary your tears were!" cried Raggedy Ann, "You might have been having a lot of fun all this time instead of crying over something which could not happen."

"That is quite true, Raggedy Ann!" the Grung laughed, "I never thought of it before." Then he sighed, "Ho! Humm! I'm hungry!"

"I do not believe we have eaten all of the goodies from the basket," mamma bear said as she opened the large picnic basket of lunch. And, this was true. For, the basket filled up immediately when anything was taken from it. It was a magic basket.

"I'll tell you what let's play," the Grung said after he had eaten all he wished from the basket. "Let's tie my tail to the limb of a tree and make a swing. Then we will play that it costs a penny to take a ride in the swing. Someone can be the penny taker and the others can take turns swinging."

Daddy bear tied the Grung's long tail to the limb of a tree and the Grung swung everyone up so high, their feet touched the leaves of the tree.

The Grung was having just as much fun as anyone else, when suddenly it grew very dark.

"My goodness!" mama bear cried, "It is clouding up to rain. Everyone run to our house so you won't get wet."

They all followed mama bear as she ran towards her house. That is, everyone except the Grung. He had his tail tied to the tree and could only run the length of his tail.

When Raggedy Ann saw the Grung in such a predicament, she ran back to untie him. But, the kind hearted wolf happened to think of the poor Grung tied to the tree, so he ran back too. Then Raggedy Andy happened to think of the Grung tied to the tree, and all the others happened to think of the Grung, so they all ran back to untie him.

There they all were, just as a great hand reached down

from the sky and lifted the Fuzzywump right up out of sight.

Daddy bear caught up baby bear, and with mama bear, hid in under some large stones. Goldilocks, Red Riding Hood and her grandmother ran for home as fast as they could go.

"Dear me!" Raggedy Ann asked of Raggedy Andy and the puppydog, "Did you ever see the like? Here we are, left alone and the poor Fuzzywump has been carried right up in the air by the big hand."

"I will never see the Fuzzywump again!" the puppydog howled as he sat down and held his nose straight up in the air.

"Please do not howl with your nose held straight up in the air," Raggedy Ann asked the puppydog. "It will not bring the Fuzzywump back and it will make your nose red."

"But I do not care to be left behind!" the puppydog cried. "I want to go wherever the Fuzzywump goes, for I am his puppydog and I shall never see him again."

Of course, Raggedy Ann and Raggedy Andy both thought this to be true. But, they knew it would do no good to tell the puppydog they thought so.

"Remember, puppydog!" Raggedy Ann said, "We are inside the Fuzzywump's magic book and have become mixed up in some of the stories. Perhaps the Fuzzywump has been lifted out of the book."

Raggedy Ann did not know why she thought this to be true, but it was just what had happened. For, presently they heard a very loud whistle, and, looking up into the sky, the Raggedys and the puppydog saw a great large face which nearly covered the entire sky and shut out most of the light.

They could see that it was the Fuzzywump's face. When the Fuzzywump saw Raggedy Ann, Raggedy Andy, and the puppydog, he reached down and lifted them out of the magic book. And, when they were out of the magic book, of course, they were as large as the Fuzzywump.

"Here is my mother!" the Fuzzywump laughed. "While she was walking through the woods, she saw the magic book lying open and when she looked in and saw me, she lifted me right out."

Mother Fuzzywump was a very nice little fat Fuzzywump mama with a cheery face and a happy twinkle in her eyes.

"Pick up your magic book, Wumpie!" she said, "And let's hurry home before my ice cream melts."

And, as everyone, even the puppydog was very hungry after such exciting adventures, they followed mama Fuzzy-

wump along the winding path through the deep woods.

"Mother Fuzzywump is so glad to see you and your funny little puppydog, I hope you will never run away from home again," Raggedy Ann said to the Fuzzywump as he dished out the ice cream.

"Indeed, I shall never run away from home again!" the Fuzzywump promised. "For I know how sad it made my darling mother without her Fuzzywump boy!"

The Fuzzywump put his arms around his nice mother and gave her a great hug.

When they had finished eating their ice cream, mother Fuzzywump said, "It is so far through the woods to the ice cream store, I believe I will start one right here in our own home so we will not have to go away to get all the ice cream we wish."

"I will get boards and nails and build a store front to our house," the Fuzzywump said, "With a nice porch where we can have pretty chairs and tables where everyone can sit and eat ice cream."

"Why not have candy covered cookies and everything like that in the store?" Raggedy Ann asked.

"And toys and games, too!" mother Fuzzywump laughed. "All of the woodland folk and little creatures like toys and games to play with on rainy days."

Raggedy Andy took the little crooked stick from his pocket and wiggled it around and everyone was startled to hear a loud noise out in front of the Fuzzywump house. When they ran out to see what caused it, they found that Raggedy Andy's wish for a fine Fuzzywump store had come true. And the store was filled with lovely books, games, toys, and everything anyone could wish.

"It is all so lovely, we shall never charge anyone for anything they buy," mother Fuzzywump said.

"That is very nice of you," Raggedy Andy said, "So I will take the little crooked stick and make another wish. I wish that whenever anything is taken from the shelf another will take its place, so the store will never run out of nice things."

Mother Fuzzywump kissed Raggedy Andy and Raggedy Ann and thanked them kindly for everything they had done for her.

Raggedy Andy handed the little crooked stick to the Fuzzywump and said, "This crooked magical stick belongs to you, Fuzzywump, so you must have it!"

"Oh, no, Raggedy Andy!" the Fuzzywump laughed, "I gave the stick to you, so it is yours."

Raggedy Ann laughed her soft cotton stuffed laugh, "Why not break the magic stick in two so that both of you can have a magical stick?"

"Probably that will break the magic of the stick," Raggedy Andy suggested.

"I do not believe so!" Raggedy Ann replied as she took the stick and snapped it in two pieces. "Now each make a wish and see!" she requested.

So, when Raggedy Andy and the Fuzzywump each made a wish, the wishes came true right away, and one part of the wishing stick was as good as the other.

Mother Fuzzywump, the Fuzzywump, and the puppydog wanted Raggedy Ann and Raggedy Andy to stay and live with them at their magic store. But Raggedy Ann said, "Thank you! but Raggedy Andy and I have been away from home so long, we must return before the folks find out we have been on such a wonderful adventure."

"You see!" Raggedy Andy explained to the Fuzzywump's nice mother, "Raggedy Ann and I are only rag dolls stuffed with nice clean white cotton, and, our little mistress,

Marcella, does not know that we can really talk and walk and have such lovely adventures. So, we always return home before she discovers we have been away."

"Then, of course, you must return home!" mother Fuzzywump sighed. "So, though we wish you would stay with us, we know how your mistress, Marcella, would miss you."

Mother Fuzzywump kissed the Raggedys a fond goodbye, the Fuzzywump hugged them goodbye, and the puppy-dog felt so sad, he held his funny little nose in the air and howled softly.

Then Raggedy Andy put his rag arms around Raggedy Ann and made a wish. And before either of them could say—Higgeldy, Piggeldy, my black hen, she lays eggs for gentlemen—the two kindly rag dolls found themselves lying on their little doll beds in the nursery, with their shoe button eyes shining up toward the ceiling and cheery happy thoughts running through their soft, cotton stuffed heads. The adventure through the Fuzzywump's magic book had ended, very happily.

JOHNNY GRUELLE-

RAGGEDY ANN
AND THE
GOLDEN BUTTERFLY

RAGGEDY ANN AND THE GOLDEN BUTTERFLY

BY

JOHNNY GRUELLE

To My Children

J. GRUELLE

Chapter One

MARCELLA and all the dollies were having a fine time at the tea party in the playhouse under the big apple tree.

They were a bit sticky from the milk, that Marcella pretended was tea, and the cake with chocolate icing.

Raggedy Ann, Uncle Clem, Beloved Belindy, and the French doll were sitting at the little table with their mistress. Percy, the policeman, who never did care much for tea parties, had been placed in a little chair on the porch. "So you can keep any stray puppydogs away," his little mistress said when she put him there.

Raggedy Andy had been fidgety at the table. He kept slipping down in his chair, so, Marcella put him on top of the toy piano in the corner. "Where you can have more room to wiggle," she said.

When the party was over, Marcella gathered up the dollies and took them in the house where they had their faces washed and their hair combed. Then they were, one by one, tucked lovingly into bed and given a good night kiss.

As she came to Raggedy Ann, Marcella stopped and looked around. "Where is Raggedy Andy?" she asked.

Raggedy Ann and Raggedy Andy slept in the large doll bed in the corner of the nursery.

"Oh, well!" Marcella said, "He will be alright in the playhouse and we can get him in the morning." She finished tucking them all in and tip-toed from the room.

Raggedy Ann did not like the idea of Raggedy Andy not being in his place next to her. "What if that big dog next door should be chasing cats during the night and wander into the playhouse?" she thought. He played so roughly and might easily harm Raggedy Andy.

Raggedy Ann wasn't a bit sleepy. She just lay there thinking for a long, long time. The house had grown very quiet. All the real-for-sure people had gone to bed and the moon was shining brightly through the nursery window.

Raggedy Ann had an idea she could think better over by the window. She got up quietly, climbed up on the chair by the window and stood with her elbows resting on the window sill. She enjoyed the fragrant night air and the lovely moonlight and there in the orchard was the playhouse with Raggedy Andy probably sound asleep.

Just outside the window was the back porch roof. Without really thinking, Raggedy Ann pulled herself up on the window sill and dropped quietly to the roof. She walked over to the corner where the rainspout went down—slid down it so easily, she hardly realized she was there on the ground. She hurried to the playhouse. Raggedy Andy was gone!

She looked everywhere, inside and out. "Raggedy Andy! Raggedy Andy!" she called softly. What could have happened to him? Where was Raggedy Andy?

She ran straight for the hole in the orchard fence where

a tiny path led to the deep, deep woods filled with fairies n' everything.

Raggedy Ann had not gone far along the path when she met Eddie Elf. "Hello, Eddie Elf!" Raggedy Ann called, "Have you seen Raggedy Andy?"

"Good Evening, Raggedy Ann!" the cheery little elf greeted, "Yes! Raggedy Andy passed by a long time ago! He seemed to be in a hurry—said he was following a beautiful Golden Butterfly and he was sure it was a good fairy. You will find him if you go right down the path."

Raggedy Ann thanked Eddie Elf and hurried on her way.

Uncle Unk closed the large account book and wiped the pen on his shirt sleeve. "Why is it we do so little business in this lovely little store?" His question was to Auntie Aunt in the next room.

"My dear!" Auntie Aunt laughed, "You forget! there really isn't any business, so, why worry about it?"

At this, Uncle Unk began crying bitterly. Auntie Aunt took off his glasses and wiped his eyes with the corner of her clean white apron. "Don't cry!" she said, "It just makes your nose red; and, after all, does no good."

"Ha, that's it! Nothing does any good! We shall al-

ways be poor! We shall never have any happiness!" Uncle Unk went on as he waved his arms about.

"Look at this store! Where will you find a nicer store? Look at the lovely books! Look at the pretty toy drums! Look at all of the other wonderful things!" Uncle Unk continued.

"I see them!" Auntie Aunt said, a little sadly, "Everything is lovely, to be sure!"

"But, can we sell any of the things?" Uncle Unk asked, —"No! Even though I have marked everything down from two pennies to one penny, no one comes in to buy." And again he burst into tears so that they splashed down upon the table and made a little puddle.

"We are so poor," he sobbed. "I cannot even buy a new pair of shoes. Look at my toes sticking out!"

"Silly, silly," Auntie Aunt chuckled, "You haven't any shoes on. No wonder your toes stick out."

Uncle Unk wiped his eyes upon his shirt sleeve and looked at his feet. He wiggled his toes and twisted his feet about. "Now where in the world can those shoes be?" he asked, "I am sure I had them on a moment ago."

"And," Auntie laughed, "I am certain you forgot to put them on this morning. There they are under your bed, just where you took them off last night. Brand new shoes they are, too." Auntie Aunt laughed her hearty laugh. "You picked them from the store shelf and fitted them yourself yesterday afternoon."

"What became of my glasses?" Uncle Unk asked as he looked about on the floor.

"You have them in your hand!" Auntie Aunt said without turning from her dusting.

Uncle Unk put on his glasses and looked about the store.

It was a cunning little store with many shelves painted

in different colors. Upon the shelves were toys and games of all kinds. Books, dolls, bicycles, trains, automobiles, and everything you could wish for. There on one shelf were many pairs of tiny shoes, no larger than doll shoes.

"HMMM!" Uncle Unk mused aloud, "How does it happen, if I took down a new pair of shoes for myself yesterday, they are still up there on the shelf?"

"Dear me, dear me, dear me!" Auntie Aunt raised her hands in a hopeless way, "You know, as well as I, Uncle Unk," she said, "When Mr. Mulligan, the magician, gave us this store; one of the things he explained to us was that everything in the store was magical. He told us when we take any of the tiny things from the shelves, the tiny thing grows to the size needed and another thing just like it takes its place upon the shelf."

Auntie Aunt looked at Uncle Unk in a puzzled sort of way and shook her head as though she was thinking, "I can't understand what has come over you."

Uncle Unk scratched his nose thoughtfully. "It's all very, very confusing," he said. "I guess I will walk down to Granny Huddle's house and see how she is getting along. She wasn't feeling so very well, you know!"

"You just whistle for your shoes, Uncle Unk," Auntie Aunt said as she wiped one of the window panes until it sparkled.

Uncle Unk turned in his chair, held his feet out toward the bed room, and whistled. One of the shoes under the bed stirred slightly and nestled up closer to the other.

"Here shoes! Here shoes!" Uncle Unk called as he snapped his fingers. Both shoes stirred slightly and wagged their tongues in a friendly sort of way. Still, they did not come out from under the bed. Uncle Unk whistled again and clapped his hands together. "Will you come out, or shall I get a stick?" he cried.

Auntie Aunt put down her dust cloth and caught up the broom. Uncle Unk's shoes quickly shuffled far back under the bed.

"Now you've frightened them and they will never come out!" Uncle Unk cried.

"We'll see about that!" Auntie Aunt said as she scuffled the broom under the bed.

The shoes came scurrying out from their hiding place and clattered in opposite directions. One to the kitchen where it shivered under a chair and the other rattling through a hole in the screen door.

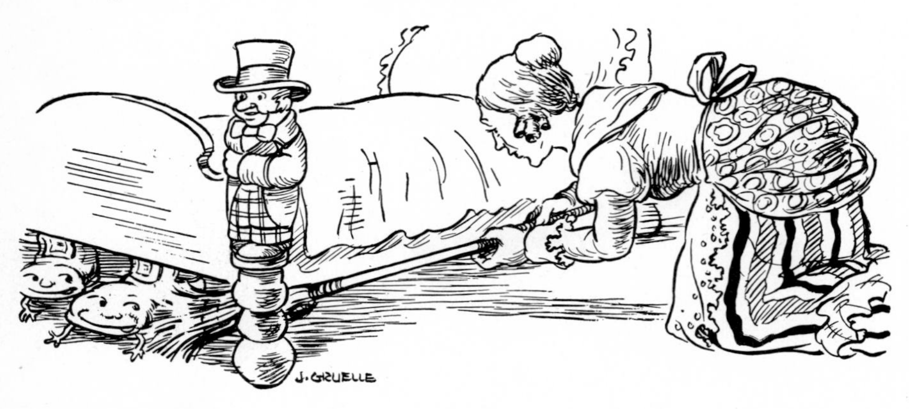

"Now you HAVE done it!" Uncle Unk sobbed. "From now on, I will only have one shoe and I suppose I will have to go barefooted the rest of my life."

Auntie Aunt went out in the kitchen and rattled the broom handle behind the chair so loudly, the shoe went hustling out of the kitchen so fast, it turned over three times. Then it slid carefully along the floor and hopped up on Uncle Unk's foot.

"They will soon learn," Auntie Aunt said. "Every new pair of shoes has to be taught." Then she brought a bottle of shoe blacking and put some upon the toe of the shoe. At this, the shoe wagged its tongue.

Uncle Unk whistled softly, for he saw the other shoe peeping through the hole in the screen door.

"It will come when it smells the shoe blacking," Auntie Aunt laughed as she returned to her dusting.

Sure enough, the shoe jumped through the hole in the screen, but, instead of hopping on to the foot without a shoe, it started bumping and striking itself against the shoe already on Uncle Unk's foot. At the first crack, Uncle Unk let out a howl and fell backward out of his chair.

Auntie Aunt came running and after much scuffling managed to catch the "wild" shoe. Then she sat right down on the floor and laughed, and laughed.

"I don't see anything funny about it," Uncle Unk cried as he rubbed his ankle.

"HA, HA, HA!" Auntie Aunt laughed as she rocked back and forth, "The first shoe was so excited when I scuffled the broom after it, it got on the wrong foot and the other shoe was trying to fight it off." With this, Auntie Aunt took off the first shoe and changed it to the right foot. Then she gave both shoes a few encouraging pats and a touch of shoe blacking.

"In another day, they will be all right," she said as she wiped Uncle Unk's eyes with the dust cloth and gave him a strawberry lollipop.

Uncle Unk ran his fingers through his hair in a puzzled sort of way. Auntie Aunt was watching him out of the corner of her eye. "You were going to walk down to Granny Huddle's house, Uncle Unk. There is your hat on the floor where it rolled when you tumbled out of your chair."

Uncle Unk wiggled his forefinger at his hat and then pointed to his head. The hat, which was a very beautiful one with colored ribbons on it, sailed into the air and came to rest in its proper place on Uncle Unk's head.

"Give this to Granny Huddle, please!" Auntie Aunt said as she handed him a brown paper bag. Then she kissed Uncle Unk goodbye and closed the screen door behind him.

Chapter Two

ISN'T he the dearest, old dear?" Auntie Aunt said aloud. When she finished dusting, Auntie Aunt put her dust cloth away and walked out into the kitchen. She took a large book from the cupboard and placed it on the table. "I wonder what Uncle Unk would like for luncheon?" Auntie Aunt mused as she sat in a comfortable chair and folded her hands. When she said this, the book opened itself and slowly turned its pages. It was a recipe book. And, a very unusual one, as you shall soon see.

"Uncle Unk is very fond of topsyturvies," the recipe book said in a low soft voice, like a radio turned low.

"Yes!" Auntie Aunt agreed, "Let us have them. Now, what else?"

"Here is a lovely recipe for snuggled, baked chicken," the book suggested.

"That would be nice!" Auntie Aunt agreed.

"Some noodle soup?" the book asked.

"Yes! noodle soup and baked biscuits," Auntie Aunt laughed.

"Now that that is settled, let us see what the weather

report is," Auntie Aunt said as she turned on the radio near her chair. . . . "The weather today will be bright and sunshiny followed by clear sunshiny weather every day the whole year through."

"I'm glad to hear that," Auntie Aunt said, "For, Uncle Unk did not wear his rubbers or take an umbrella. And I would not like him to be caught in a shower and get his pretty hat and new shoes all wet."

"No fear of that, Auntie Aunt," the soft voice of the radio was saying. "Now would you like news of the day, luncheon music, or a play?"

"Thank you!" Auntie Aunt replied, "If we may have some music when we are having luncheon, it will be nice. But just now I am too busy to sit and listen. Will you please excuse me if I turn you off?"

"Oh, yes indeed, Auntie Aunt!" the radio voice laughed. "We are just about to broadcast the voice of a lady who gives out recipes every morning at this time. And, of course, everyone turns off the radio then. Goodbye!"

"Thank you, goodbye!" Auntie Aunt said cheerily as she snapped off the radio and started out of the door.

"Excuse me a moment?" the radio voice came on again. "What time would you like the luncheon music, Auntie Aunt?"

"Just as soon as the recipe lady signs off," said Auntie.

Auntie Aunt walked out into the garden to pick a bouquet of flowers and gather a few wild cream puffs which grew near the garden wall.

She knew she would not have to worry about luncheon, for the magical recipe book would take care of everything. Indeed, as Auntie Aunt went about the garden, she could

hear the book giving orders to the flour to sift itself; the sugar to measure out sixteen spoonfulls; the chicken to cuddle in the roasting pan.

Yes, it was a remarkable book. Everyone should have one in the kitchen. It makes things so much easier. Everything works by magic rules. Nothing is ever overcooked. Pies never, never bubble over the sides of the pie pans and burn in the oven.

When Auntie Aunt heard the radio start playing softly, she took the flowers and cream puffs into the dining room. Luncheon had placed itself carefully upon the table and the chairs had drawn themselves up to their proper places.

"Why, mercy sakes!" Auntie Aunt cried. Her chair was at its place but Uncle Unk's chair remained back against the wall. "Now, you lazy thing!" Auntie Aunt cried, shaking her finger at Uncle Unk's chair. "You get right up to your place at the table and be quick about it! What will Uncle Unk think?"

The chair waggled itself from side to side like a boy who has misbehaved and is ashamed, but it did not walk up to the table.

Auntie Aunt took hold of the chair and rattled its legs

against the floor as she pulled it to the table while the chair held back as best it could.

"There!" Auntie Aunt cried, a little out of breath as she thumped the chair's four legs in place at the table, "Don't you ever try that again, or I will get a new chair from the store shelf to take your place!"

Just then the little bell above the store door tinkled. And, as Auntie Aunt walked into the store, Uncle Unk's chair tilted itself upon its front legs and quietly tiptoed back to its place near the wall.

Auntie Aunt was surprised to see what, at first glance, she thought was a little girl, standing in the store. It had been a long time since anyone had come to buy anything.

"Good morning, my dear!" Auntie Aunt said, "May I help you?"

"It is such a cunning little store, I thought you would

not mind if I came in and looked around," the little stranger answered.

"No indeed!" Auntie Aunt laughed, "We are delighted to see you! Who are you, my dear?"

"I am Raggedy Ann!" the little stranger replied as if that told all about herself.

"Oh, to be sure!" Auntie Aunt exclaimed, "I have heard and read about you and have seen your pictures. I thought I knew you."

"Yes!" Raggedy Ann continued, "I am just a cheerful old rag doll stuffed with nice fluffy white cotton and with a candy heart with 'I LOVE YOU' written upon it."

"You do not live around here, do you?" Auntie Aunt asked in her kindliest tone.

"Well, I don't know just how far away it is," Raggedy Ann replied. "But I live with my little mistress, Marcella, and all the other dolls, and our home is right on the edge of the deep, deep woods. I started out last night to search for my brother and best friend, Raggedy Andy, who is lost."

"You look rather tired, my dear," Auntie Aunt said. "You must come in and rest and have luncheon with us. Uncle Unk will be home any minute now and we will help you find Raggedy Andy."

"You are so kind. Thank you, Missus, ah—Missus—" Raggedy Ann hesitated.

"I am Auntie Aunt, not Missus, please! Now will you come?" Auntie Aunt asked as she held out her hand.

"Yes, thank you!" Raggedy Ann smiled her best cottony smile as she took Auntie Aunt's hand and the two walked into the dining room.

"I wonder if Uncle Unk could have stopped in the garden to eat some cream puffs?" Auntie Aunt said to Raggedy Ann as she went to the door and looked out.

"The chair! the chair!" Auntie Aunt cried as she pointed to Uncle Unk's chair back against the wall. "It has never acted that way before. Now I know something has happened to Uncle Unk. He likes to sit beside the brook and watch the fish, and has forgotten it is lunch time."

"I will put on my bonnet, if you will excuse me, Raggedy Ann, and go and find him. It will only take a minute. You sit right down and start your luncheon!"

"I had better go with you! Perhaps I can help?" Raggedy Ann suggested.

"Oh, no! you just rest and enjoy yourself and I will be back in a jiffy," Auntie Aunt was saying as she hurried out the back door.

Raggedy Ann was not very hungry, so she sat down in a comfortable chair to await the return of Auntie Aunt and, she hoped, Uncle Unk.

In just a little while, it seemed, Auntie Aunt was back. "I cannot imagine where Uncle Unk has wandered this time," she said. "He has not been to Granny Huddle's house and he is not beside the brook, where I so often find him. Well, let us go ahead with luncheon and we will both go and look for Uncle Unk.

"Does Uncle Unk get lost often?" Raggedy Ann asked.

"Just about every time he goes out," Auntie Aunt laughingly replied.

When Auntie Aunt and Raggedy Ann finished their luncheon, the dishes carried themselves into the kitchen and snuggled into the dishpan. The hot water turned on and filled the dishpan; the soap slid from its dish and stirred up white suds; and a dish rag mopped off the dishes. Each dish, as it was washed, held itself under the hot water faucet and rinsed itself of soapsuds then carefully took its place in a drainer.

Raggedy Ann watched in amazement, "It is just like invisible hands doing everything. Isn't it, Auntie Aunt?"

"Yes indeed!" Auntie Aunt laughed, "It was a great surprise to us when we first came, but, now we never think of the magic that causes the wonderful things around here."

Auntie Aunt led the way into the store and asked Raggedy Ann to pick out a lovely new dress and apron; for the ones she wore had been soiled and torn in her trip through the deep, deep woods.

"Oh, but Auntie Aunt—!" Raggedy Ann exclaimed as she saw all the beautiful things.

"It is just what Uncle Unk would wish me to do," Auntie Aunt laughed.

"You know, I always wear the same kind of dress and apron, Auntie Aunt," Raggedy Ann said, "And I'll just bet you haven't any like this."

"Of course we have!" Auntie Aunt smiled, "In this magic store we have anything you wish."

Auntie Aunt took a dozen, or so, dresses and several crisp white aprons from the shelf. And, would you believe it? They were exactly the style Raggedy Ann always wears.

"How shall I ever repay you and Uncle Unk?" Raggedy Ann wondered.

"Oh, Raggedy Ann!" Auntie Aunt said cheerily, "There are many ways, of course, but one does not expect payment for an act of kindness.

"Now let us go and see if we can find Uncle Unk," Raggedy Ann suggested.

"Yes, let's!" agreed Auntie Aunt, "For the poor dear has probably forgotten where he was going."

"And, perhaps he has forgotten the way back home," Raggedy Ann added.

As they started away, Auntie Aunt wiped a tear from her eye and said, "Perhaps the old darling is sitting somewhere in the deep wood on a cold hard stone not knowing what to do. We must find him."

Chapter Three

IF WE only had a nice puppydog, he could probably lead us right to where Uncle Unk is sitting upon the hard cold stone," Raggedy Ann said.

"But, we haven't a puppydog, Raggedy Ann!" Auntie Aunt said with regret. Then she happened to think, "We have some nice toy puppydogs in the store, but they would not do. We need a real-for-sure live puppydog, not one stuffed with cotton or sawdust."

"May I run in the store and get a toy puppydog to try, Auntie Aunt?" Raggedy Ann asked.

"Yes, my dear!" Auntie Aunt sobbed.

"Now do not worry about Uncle Unk," Raggedy Ann said as she wiped away Auntie Aunt's tears, "We'll find him in a few minutes."

Raggedy Ann ran quickly to the store and came back carrying a tiny toy puppydog.

"I wouldn't worry so much about Uncle Unk if the poor dear would not get so hungry," Auntie Aunt said, "But when Uncle Unk left the store to go to Granny Huddle's, all he had in a paper bag was nine cream puffs, a jelly roll, eight chocolate cookies, some fried chicken, and four buttered biscuits which he was supposed to take to Granny Huddle."

"Oh, then he will be all right!" Raggedy Ann said. "If he gets hungry he can eat the things in the paper bag."

"That's what worries me," Auntie Aunt cried, the tears streaming down her cheeks. "Uncle Unk would forget in five minutes he was to take the things to Granny, and would sit down and eat them himself. So by now, he must be very hungry."

"Here's the toy puppydog," Raggedy Ann said as she put the little creature on the ground. "Now I will see if I can get the little fellow to work for us."

Auntie Aunt sat down on the soft grass at the side of the garden path while Raggedy Ann drew a circle in the dust of the path. Raggedy Ann carefully placed the toy puppydog in the center of the circle and walked around the circle three times while she was making a wish on her Wishing Pebble. Then Raggedy Ann placed both hands over her eyes and walked backward around the circle as she sang, "Hippity-hop to the Barber Shop." She reached down then,

patted the puppydog and said, "I'll name you Millicent."

"Thank you!" the puppydog barked as he jumped up and frisked around, "It is a lovely name."

"Millicent! do you think you can find Uncle Unk?" Auntie Aunt asked.

"I can if he is on the ground," Millicent replied, "But, if he has gone up in an aeroplane, I will not be able to follow him. Do you know?" Millicent continued, "I can smell cream puffs, jelly roll, fried chicken and other nice things. Do you think Uncle Unk smelled like that?"

"Those were the things Auntie Aunt put in the bag Uncle Unk carried," Raggedy Ann said.

"Then follow me!" Millicent barked in a sawdusty voice, "And I will lead you to where he is, if he is still there."

"If he is still there he must be there, Millicent," Raggedy Ann laughed.

"Don't be too certain of that!" Millicent replied as she trotted down the path in the opposite direction from Granny Huddle's house.

"No wonder I could not find Uncle Unk," Auntie Aunt said with surprise, "I thought he had gone toward Granny's."

Millicent trotted along down the road. "Uncle Unk stopped here and ate some cream puffs," Millicent said, "I know he did because I can smell the crumbs." She trotted on.

"Uncle Unk sat on this stone and ate the fried chicken and biscuits," Millicent said as she ran around a large stone.

"Ha!" Millicent cried after she had sniffed all around the stone, "Something happened here. Either Uncle Unk has been chased or he is chasing something, for, he has started running as fast as he can run."

Millicent now left the road and trotted through the bushes and ferns into the deep woods.

"I hope whatever was chasing Uncle Unk did not catch him," Auntie Aunt cried as she and Raggedy Ann followed Millicent as closely as they could.

"If something was chasing him, it was up in the air," Millicent said. "If it was on the ground, I would smell it."

Millicent zigzagged this way and that, crisscrossing the

trail a great many times, until she finally came to a brook.

"There, you see!" she said as she sat down on the bank, "That is what I meant when I said I would lead you to where he is if he is still there, and . . . here he isn't."

"We can see that Uncle Unk is not here, Millicent," Raggedy Ann said, "You must hunt farther along the bank of the brook."

"No use," Millicent said, "Uncle Unk must have gone up in the air and forgot to come down."

"Oh, Millicent!" Auntie Aunt cried, "Uncle Unk couldn't do that, you know."

"No, I do not know!" Millicent insisted, "I just know that, here he is not."

"Oh, look! There is his hat on the other side of the brook," Auntie Aunt cried. "Uncle Unk must have crossed the brook. Oh, dear! I do hope he took off his new shoes. If he gets them wet, they will squeak like rusty hinges every step he takes."

Auntie Aunt took off her shoes and stockings but Raggedy Ann just skipped across the little brook holding Millicent in her arms.

When Millicent got to the ground again, she had hardly

taken one little teeny-weeny sniff, when she said, "Yes! there is Uncle Unk's hat and I can tell he is still running."

Raggedy Ann and Millicent waited while Auntie Aunt put on her shoes and stockings. Then, with Millicent showing the way, they again followed the trail that was taking them deeper and deeper into the woods.

Presently they came to a place where a very crooked path led away from the trail. Millicent sniffed and sniffed and then started along the crooked path with Auntie Aunt

and Raggedy Ann right behind her. They had not gone far when they came to a very strange looking little house.

The house had only one room and a tall crooked chimney was built at the side. It stood upon a little hill in a clearing in the deep woods.

Millicent trotted straight up to the door and stopped. She sniffed there for a moment, then ran around the house and stood looking in the open door. "There, you see!" she cried, "There he isn't, again!"

"But, he must be!" Raggedy Ann said.

"If he is, where is he?" Millicent wanted to know.

"I know, maybe Uncle Unk is sitting on the roof," Auntie Aunt suggested. But when they looked up toward

the roof, it was easy to see that he was not there at all.

"Uncle Unk's hat is wiggling in my hands," Auntie Aunt remarked, "Just as though it wanted to go to Uncle Unk's head. So, Uncle Unk must be close by."

Auntie Aunt explained, "The hat is magical like all of the things in Uncle Unk's store. If Uncle Unk is close by, the hat will sail up in the air and come down just right on Uncle Unk's head. Just as Uncle Unk's shoes scuffle along the floor and put themselves on for him if he is not too far away."

"Do not hold the hat, Auntie Aunt," Raggedy Ann suggested.

Auntie Aunt let go of the hat and while they all watched, the hat sailed slowly into the air, through the door and came to rest above a rocking chair.

"He is not there. We can see that very plainly," Raggedy Ann said.

Auntie Aunt sat down upon the front step and cried very softly.

"Uncle Unk is either there or, as I said before, he isn't," Millicent cried.

"Uncle Unk is sitting in that empty rocking chair," Raggedy Ann seemed sure. "He is invisible to us and we are invisible to him. We must be very, very careful or we will find ourselves under the same spell as Uncle Unk."

"If Uncle Unk is invisible and is sitting in that rocking chair, I shall go in and feel all about and rescue him," Auntie Aunt cried as she wiped her eyes and jumped up from the step.

Raggedy Ann put her hand on Auntie Aunt's arm, "I wouldn't step inside, Auntie Aunt!" she said.

"If dear Uncle Unk is in there, I wish to know it!" Auntie Aunt cried.

"Take Raggedy Ann's advice," Millicent said, "You may regret going in the house."

But Auntie Aunt had already stepped across the door-sill. Raggedy Ann and Millicent watched breathlessly from outside the strange little magical house. They saw Auntie Aunt walk across the room to the rocking chair. Auntie Aunt felt all around the chair and then turned to her friends outside and said something. And, although they could see Auntie Aunt's lips move, they could not hear a sound.

"Her voice has become invisible," Raggedy Ann whispered. "But I could tell from the way her lips moved that she said, 'Uncle Unk is in the chair.' "

"See how transparent she is growing. I can see the wall right through Auntie Aunt," Millicent cried.

"Oh, dear!" Raggedy Ann whispered, "She has gone."

Raggedy Ann stepped back from the door and pulled Millicent with her.

When Auntie Aunt walked through the door of the strange little house, she felt no different than had she walked through the door of any other house.

Auntie Aunt walked over to the rocking chair and felt about. She could feel Uncle Unk sitting there but she could not see him. Auntie Aunt turned towards the doorway and said, "Uncle Unk is in the chair." Then, to her great surprise, as she looked at Raggedy Ann and Millicent, they seemed to gradually fade away and become invisible.

"Look!" Auntie Aunt cried, "They have disappeared completely."

"Who disappeared?" it was the voice of Uncle Unk asking.

Auntie Aunt turned and then she saw Uncle Unk sitting

in the chair. His hands and feet were tied with ropes. Auntie Aunt quickly untied him. "What happened?" she asked as she hugged him and gave him a big kiss.

"When?" Uncle Unk asked in reply.

"You left the store to walk to Granny Huddle's house this morning," Auntie Aunt explained. "See, you still have the bag in your hand which you were to take to Granny."

"Dear me!" Uncle Unk cried, "Why should I take my hand to Granny, when she has two hands of her own?"

"Silly!" Auntie Aunt laughed, "Not your hand! I meant the bag full of cream puffs, jelly roll, and other goodies."

"My dear! the bag contains no jelly roll, cream puffs, fried chicken, or biscuits. See for yourself!" And he held the bag open so that Auntie Aunt could see inside.

"You have eaten everything!" she smiled. "Now, Uncle Unk, try to remember just what you did. We want to know just what happened."

"I lost my hat. I can remember that," Uncle Unk went on. "I will be glad when I find it again. My head feels so funny without a hat."

Auntie Aunt did not tell him his hat was on his head at that very moment. Instead, she asked, "What were you doing when you lost your hat?"

"Oh!" Uncle Unk cried, jumping from his chair, "I remember now. I was running after a golden butterfly. A beautiful golden butterfly. Its wings were of solid gold and shone in the sunshine just like a bright new penny. I must hurry and follow it until I find out where it lives. Then we will find many more like it, all gold. And we will be rich with all the gold we wish."

Uncle Unk started to run out the door, but when he reached it he seemed to strike something and was thrown back into the room and bumped his head on the floor.

Uncle Unk howled dismally while Auntie Aunt rubbed his head.

Then Auntie Aunt walked over to the door and felt around in the opening. Something which felt like rubber was stretched across the opening. Auntie Aunt tried to walk through the door but she found she could not do it.

When Uncle Unk's howling had quieted, Auntie Aunt said, "We are prisoners in this strange house. And, not only that, we are invisible to our friends outside. We can see each other but we cannot see them. What shall we do?"

"Let us have some food," Uncle Unk suggested.

"There is nothing to eat here, Uncle Unk!" Auntie Aunt told him. "Some day I shall lose patience with you and I'll put you across my knee and give you a good paddling. If you had gone to Granny's as you started out to do, we would not have been in this pickle."

"I wish that I had a pickle. A dill pickle and a piece of bread and butter," Uncle Unk sighed.

"Well, you will not get any!" Auntie Aunt told him as she sat down in another rocker and folded her hands. "If we cannot escape from this house, we will just have to wait until we are rescued."

"That is quite true!" Uncle Unk agreed. So, he just sat down in a chair and folded his hands, too.

Chapter Four

RAGGEDY ANN and Millicent sat back in under some bushes where they could watch the door of the house. They were very quiet but Millicent finally broke the silence with a low sawdusty growl as she turned her head to look down the path.

Raggedy Ann was about to get to her feet when she looked and saw a young man walking quietly down the path in their direction. She could scarcely believe her eyes. It was Raggedy Andy!

"Hello, hello, hello! I certainly never thought I would find you here!" Raggedy Andy was saying as he ran up and gave Raggedy Ann a big hug.

Millicent sat back on the grass wondering what this was all about when Raggedy Ann called her over and introduced her to Raggedy Andy.

Both Ann and Andy were busy for several minutes explaining how each happened to be in this strange place so far from home.

"I was sound asleep on top of the toy piano in the playhouse," Raggedy Andy explained, "When suddenly I was awakened and thought it was daylight. I sat up and looked around. It was still night outside with the moon shining brightly. Waking suddenly like that, I was rather dull and it took me a little minute before I saw, there on the edge of the playhouse tea table, a beautiful Golden Butterfly; so brilliant that, at first glance, I thought it was an electric light. I got down very quietly from the piano and went over to catch it. The Golden Butterfly fluttered its wings and flew rather slowly out the door. It stopped on one of the little bushes just outside the playhouse and, just as I was going to pick it up very carefully, away it went again. This is strange, I thought. I had never seen a butterfly as beautiful as this. I will follow it, for, it must be a wonderful fairy or something. So, I have kept on following the Golden Butterfly right to here."

"Several times," Raggedy Andy continued, "I have been so close I could almost touch its wing. Just a few moments ago it was flying just above me and then it started more rapidly toward this strange little house. Now that I have come this far, I am more sure than ever it is a fairy and I must catch up with it and find out."

When Raggedy Andy finished his story, Raggedy Ann told how she had started in search of him and how she had met Auntie Aunt and they both were hunting Uncle Unk.

"Now we can help each other," Raggedy Ann said. "Oh, yes!" Raggedy Andy replied, "We will have a grand adventure!"

Then he asked, "You were not thinking of going inside that funny little house, were you?"

"No, indeed," Raggedy Ann replied, "We have just lost one good friend, Auntie Aunt, who went inside. Isn't it a strange house?"

"Very," Andy agreed, "The house must be under some sort of magic spell."

"I was just thinking the same thing a moment before you came along," Raggedy Ann said. "Perhaps we could break the spell by tearing down the strange little house. It doesn't look very strong."

"Perhaps," said Raggedy Andy, "But if we do that, who knows but that we might be tearing down a wonderful experience for those who are inside. They may be under the spell of Imagination."

"Our good friend, Auntie Aunt, did not wish to enter the door," Raggedy Ann said, "And, I really believe she is waiting as patiently as possible for us to rescue her. The magic of Imagination may at times be very lovely, when one imagines beautiful melodies, lovely thoughts, or kindly deeds; but, when the magic of Imagination is forced upon one who is not strong enough to escape, the experience is likely not to be a pleasing or beautiful adventure."

Raggedy Andy looked thoughtfully at Raggedy Ann and said, "You speak like a very wise person, Raggedy Ann. We must plan the best way to rescue your friend, Auntie Aunt, as quickly as possible. I believe, since I have been looking at this strange little house more closely, that your idea of taking it apart is a good one. And it should not be

very hard to do. Doesn't it look as though the roof had been set upon the four walls without any nails or fastenings of any kind?"

"Let's see if we can find a ladder around behind the house," Raggedy Ann suggested as she started off with Raggedy Andy and Millicent close behind her.

Sure enough, there at the back of the house, they found a ladder and Raggedy Ann cried, "That proves to me we are all under the magic spell of Imagination. And, now that we have the imagined ladder, we can climb up on the roof and slide down the chimney."

Millicent laughed, "Like the wolf did in the story of 'The Three Little Pigs.' " They laughed so at this, they were all out of breath when they finally had the ladder propped against the side of the house.

"Now, Raggedy Andy," Raggedy Ann suggested, "You can climb up and lift the roof and topple it off. Then we can pull down the four walls. I imagine that will let all of the magic leak out, like water out of a broken bottle. You see," she added, "Auntie Aunt became invisible only after she had stepped inside the house, so, I believe all the magic is on the inside."

"I think you are right," Raggedy Andy said as he started carefully up the ladder.

He found that he could lift the roof easily. And, sliding it this way and that, he finally gave one big push and the roof came toppling to the ground.

"It wasn't any heavier than cardboard," he said as he came down the ladder.

Raggedy Ann caught hold of a water spout and ripped it from the house, then she and Andy pulled one wall over.

They walked around the house pulling and pushing at each wall in turn until the walls were all flat on the ground.

"I don't see your friend," Raggedy Andy said, "Maybe she has flown away on the magic of Imagination."

The Raggedys and Millicent could see two chairs and a table standing upon the floor of the house. Then, as they watched, Auntie Aunt began to appear. "How strange!" Raggedy Andy remarked.

"Yes, that's Auntie Aunt!" Raggedy Ann cried. "Hello, Auntie Aunt! And now that must be Uncle Unk, who is getting much plainer. Can you see us?" she called.

"I imagine they can come out now," Millicent laughed.

"We were just waiting for you to show up plainly," Auntie Aunt said, as she and Uncle Unk stepped from the floor of the house and walked up to their rescuers.

Auntie Aunt introduced Uncle Unk to Raggedy Ann and Millicent and Raggedy Ann presented Raggedy Andy to both Uncle Unk and Auntie Aunt and they all felt as though they had known each other always.

"I just remember why I went into the funny house," Uncle Unk cried excitedly, "I saw the most beautiful Golden Butterfly, and I must find him or I shall never be happy again."

Just then the butterfly, which had been invisible, along with the others inside the house, fluttered up into the air, circled about, and then flew over the tree tops and out of sight. When Uncle Unk saw the butterfly, he tried his best to catch it, but it quickly flew away and was gone.

"Follow it! Follow it!" Uncle Unk cried as he dashed through the bushes with Raggedy Ann, Auntie Aunt, Raggedy Andy and Millicent trailing close behind him.

Millicent barked with joy, for every puppydog loves a chase.

"Now the Golden Butterfly has gone forever!" Uncle Unk cried when he and the others came to the brink of a high cliff and watched the butterfly until it disappeared high in the air across the lower country. "Now I shall never find contentment or happiness. If I was only young again, I would climb down the cliff and follow the Golden Butterfly until I caught it."

"Perhaps, if you caught it, Uncle Unk, you would still wish for something else," Raggedy Ann said. "Very few people are ever truly satisfied, you know!"

"And those who are satisfied are the ones who no longer have any ambition," Raggedy Andy added.

"Look!" Raggedy Ann cried as she pointed far across the valley to mountains rising high in the distance, "The clouds have rolled away from that mountain peak and there is a wonderful castle, high in the air. Can you see it shining there at the end of the lovely rainbow?"

"At the end of the rainbow!" Uncle Unk cried, "That must be the Castle of Contentment! I'll go there and find the pot of gold. I am sure that is where the Golden Butterfly lives."

"Uncle Unk!" Auntie Aunt said softly, "We have already come much too far. Let us return to our little store, if we can ever find our way back to it. We do not need the Golden Butterfly, nor the pot of gold."

"I shall never return to that dingy little place without

the Golden Butterfly and the pot of gold. How can anyone be happy without riches?" Uncle Unk cried, walking to the brink of the cliff and looking over. "See! there is a path leading down the cliff. It leads to the Castle of Contentment, and I shall take it!" And, before the others could stop him, Uncle Unk started down the steep path and disappeared in a cloud of dust and loose stones as he went slipping and sliding down the side of the mountain.

"What shall we do?" Auntie Aunt cried, and she would have jumped after Uncle Unk if Raggedy Ann had not held her by the arm.

"I can see Uncle Unk getting to his feet way down below," Raggedy Andy said. "Now he is running down the level path at the bottom. Let us search for the beginning of the path here at the top and follow him."

When Uncle Unk plunged over the cliff, Millicent had run along the top, and now she came barking back to her friends. "I have found the path," she said, "Follow me!"

The path was very steep and led along the side of the cliff to where Uncle Unk had started down. They could see where his shoes had scuffed up the loose stones and dirt as he ran along. "He wasn't injured," Millicent said, "For he is running. I can tell by the long strides he has taken."

As Raggedy Ann followed by Auntie Aunt and Raggedy

Andy rounded a sharp bend, the path ran directly into a dark grotto. Raggedy Ann came to a stop and tried to see inside. "It may lead to a volcano," she said.

"All of you wait here!" Millicent said, "I can see in the dark, so, if it is a volcano, I will return and tell you."

"I know that I shall never see Uncle Unk again," Auntie Aunt cried, as she sat down and buried her face in her apron. "Why, oh why didn't I tie Uncle Unk with a clothes line, so that he could never have come on this wild goose chase?"

Raggedy Ann thought this might have been a good plan, but she did not say so.

Millicent came trotting back towards them. "The path leads far into the side of the cliff," she said, "And away off I could see brilliant lights."

Raggedy Ann took Auntie Aunt's hand and followed by Raggedy Andy, they cautiously felt their way along the narrow path.

"There are the lights!" Raggedy Ann cried suddenly, "They reflect on the opposite side of the grotto."

Just before our friends reached the bend in the path, beyond which the light came, they heard the sound of a deep voice saying, "Stop, and consider before you enter here. This is the place from which there is no escape. He who

comes within the enchantment of vain desires, can never again be contented elsewhere. Retrace your steps before it is too late."

"Let us turn back!" Raggedy Ann cried, as she clung to Raggedy Andy's arm. "I do not like it here!"

"I shall not turn back!" Auntie Aunt insisted. "If you are afraid, you may turn back but I shall go on until I find Uncle Unk."

"Auntie Aunt, please do not go on. It is foolish," Raggedy Ann advised.

"Nothing shall stop me!" Auntie Aunt cried, "I do not seek the Golden Butterfly, nor the pot of gold, but I would never forgive myself if I did not follow Uncle Unk."

"Ah!" the deep voice said sadly, "The wise are often led by the foolish. Turn Back! Turn back!"

"I shall find Uncle Unk!" Auntie Aunt again cried. "I am not afraid. Let me go first!" And with this, she pushed ahead of Raggedy Ann and hurried around the bend of the path and out of sight of the others.

For a few moments Raggedy Ann and Raggedy Andy hesitated, then Raggedy Andy said, "Perhaps we should follow!"

"Yes!" Raggedy Ann agreed, "Uncle Unk has, through

his desire for happiness and contentment, led us this far. And though we may think him very foolish, we cannot leave Auntie Aunt to find and help him, all by herself. If her love for poor Uncle Unk can make her brave the dangers of this grotto, then my love for Auntie Aunt will make me brave whatever dangers there may be for her."

"And, I will follow you, wherever you go," Raggedy Andy said.

"Turn back! Turn back!" the deep voice again warned, "No matter how much you may love another, the spell of the

enchantment will be cast upon you and there is no escape. This is the Grotto of Greed! The Grotto of Greed!"

The great voice ended in a deep sigh, as Raggedy Ann and Andy, arm in arm, with Millicent just ahead, walked around the bend in the path and saw a beautiful building which seemed to be carved from the side of the cliff.

In front of the building, the path widened and it was lighted with hundreds of brilliant lights. Auntie Aunt was nowhere to be seen. "She has gone inside," Millicent whispered as they all walked up to the beautiful entrance.

A tall, stately lady came to greet them. "Welcome to our castle!" she said. "Whatever you may see within, you may take even though it belongs to another. There are no laws. Enter and take!"

Just before Raggedy Ann and Andy and Millicent entered the great door of the castle, they turned as if for a farewell look back along the path. When they did so, Raggedy Ann caught Raggedy Andy's arm and gasped, "The beautiful lady, look! She was attractive from the front but is ugly from the back."

"Ah!" the great voice said softly, "Greed paints the surface in bright colors, but within the hollow shell, when one has obtained a selfish desire, there is nothing but the ugliness and misery gained at the cost of virtue."

"Oh, Great Voice!" Raggedy Ann pleaded, "We came only to help our friends. Will you please assist us?"

"I am the voice in every heart which gives good advice. Those with hearts filled with generosity, tolerance, love and friendliness, know that I speak for good. Those who are led by selfish longings and foolish cravings, close the doors of their hearts and listen not to my promptings."

"We know just what you are, Great Voice, and we shall follow your advice," Raggedy Ann said.

"Let your hearts be your guides," the Great Soft Voice said, "Touch nothing that is offered within the Grotto of Greed. Accept nothing, for, everything here has been obtained through loss to another. I shall be with you always."

Chapter Five

OUR friends came to where a great room opened at the side of the castle hall. Rich tapestries threaded with gold and trimmed with sparkling jewels hung from the windows. A great crowd was bowing before a thin, weak looking king, who was seated upon a golden throne. His eyes were hollow and his face tired and worn. "Look!" Raggedy Ann whispered, "Everyone is smiling and bowing to the king, but as soon as he looks away from them, they laugh and make fun of him."

A large fat man dressed in gorgeous clothing and wearing great jewels upon his breast came up to Raggedy Ann and Raggedy Andy. He held out a tray of rings, necklaces, gold coins, and jewels toward them. "I am the Treasurer of King Teeny the Great," he said by way of introduction, "Take of these presents from his majesty and bow before him. He craves power, the silly thing. See how the courtiers fawn before him. They despise him, just as I do, but they accept his presents. Help yourselves! Here is a very beautiful necklace of diamonds which would look lovely on you," the Treasurer said to Raggedy Ann. "And this for you!" he said holding up a large emerald ring before Raggedy Andy.

"No, thank you!" Raggedy Ann and Raggedy Andy both said together.

"Then you had better walk on," the Treasurer advised. "The silly king may discover that you do not accept his presents and do not bow before him and do him homage, and may send his guards to do you harm."

Our friends walked away from the throne room of the silly king and down the great hallway. At the far end they came upon Uncle Unk. He was sitting on the floor surrounded by a great heap of golden coins. Auntie Aunt sat over at one side, her eyes filled with tears. "I cannot get Uncle Unk away from the gold," she sobbed. "He piles it up, then scatters it around, then piles it up again."

"Look! Look!" Uncle Unk cried, "I am rich. Look at the gold! It is all mine! The man said I could have as much as I wished. I shall have him bring more soon. See it glitter! Listen to it chinking! You must all help me carry it home so that I may buy everything I wish. But, I shall never return to that tiny store again. I am rich now, and shall build a beautiful castle for my very own."

The big, fat Treasurer came walking up followed by three slaves carrying great trays heaped high with golden coins. "Ah!" he said with a smile to Raggedy Ann and Raggedy Andy, "Would you like to be rich, too?"

"Oh, no!" Uncle Unk cried as he jumped to his feet, "They do not wish it! They are just friends come to help me carry the gold home. The gold is mine. All mine to do with just as I please."

"Ah, yes!" the Treasurer said as he turned away.

"Bring more presently!" Uncle Unk cried to him.

"What can we do with him?" Auntie Aunt sobbed.

"Let us go over to one side and talk it over," Raggedy Ann suggested as she took Raggedy Andy's hand and led the way to the side of the room where great pillars of sparkling stones hid them from Auntie Aunt and Uncle Unk.

"There is only one thing to do," Raggedy Andy said,

"Drag Uncle Unk out of the Grotto of Greed by force. We must try not to hurt him when we do it."

"Can't we tie his hands and feet and carry him out?" Raggedy Ann asked.

Just then our friends heard Auntie Aunt scream, and running back to her, they found that she had fainted and was lying beside Uncle Unk. Three large fierce looking men had just scooped up the golden coins in baskets and were running away. Uncle Unk had a large lump forming on top of his head where he had been struck by the man who carried a large club.

"Now is our chance!" Raggedy Andy cried, "Let us get him out of here before he recovers his senses. Raggedy Ann, will you help Auntie Aunt while Millicent and I try to find a way out of this terrible Grotto of Greed?" And, so saying, Raggedy Andy picked up Uncle Unk and lifted him to his shoulder. And with Millicent leading the way they disappeared beyond the sparkling pillars.

Raggedy Ann patted Auntie Aunt's face and shook her gently, "Wake up, Auntie Aunt!" she said.

Presently Auntie Aunt opened her eyes and looked about. "Where is Uncle Unk?" she asked.

"Hurry, Auntie Aunt, we must follow them before they get too far," Raggedy Ann said as she helped Auntie Aunt to her feet and with a firm hold of her arm started in the direction Raggedy Andy and Millicent had gone with Uncle Unk.

It was all very confusing. There were so many hallways and rooms that Raggedy Ann did not know which way her friends had gone. So many people were coming and going, counting their money, and showing their jewels. Some in groups were wrangling fiercely among themselves. Raggedy Ann finally stopped, "We have lost them, Auntie Aunt," she said, "Or rather, they have lost us."

While they were wondering what to do next, they heard Millicent barking in the distance and, in a moment, she came bounding up to them. "You took the wrong hallway," Millicent said. "Follow me and I will lead you to Raggedy Andy."

"Isn't Uncle Unk with him?" Auntie Aunt asked anxiously.

"Oh, yes!" Millicent sighed, "And he is quite safe.

J. GRUELLE.

Millicent trotted in front and led them through the laughing, quarreling groups until she came to a tiny door. "Raggedy Andy and Uncle Unk are just outside," Millicent said. "Will you please help me open the door? It is heavy."

Raggedy Ann helped Millicent push the tiny door open and they all passed through, but it was a tight squeeze for Auntie Aunt.

They were out upon the path again. It wound along the side of the cliff and down into a pleasant valley. Raggedy Andy and Uncle Unk were nowhere in sight.

"Don't worry," Millicent told Auntie Aunt, "I can follow them."

Millicent sniffed rapidly along followed closely by Auntie Aunt and Raggedy Ann. "I suppose Raggedy Andy thought it best to get Uncle Unk as far away from the Grotto of Greed as possible," Millicent said.

In just a short time they saw Raggedy Andy, and, as they came up, there was Uncle Unk sitting on the ground holding his head and looking very sad.

"How do you feel, Uncle Unk?" Auntie Aunt asked as she sat down beside him and put her arms around him.

"Hungry!" Uncle Unk replied.

"It has been a long time since we have had any food," Auntie Aunt laughed.

"I found something over in that clump of bushes," Millicent said as she came trotting toward Raggedy Ann.

"What was it?" Raggedy Ann asked.

"I never saw anything like them before," Millicent went on, "maybe you can tell me what they are."

Everyone, even Uncle Unk, who hoped it was food, followed Millicent through the bushes. "Shh, don't make any noise!" Millicent whispered.

Raggedy Ann had to chuckle to herself when she peeped through the bushes, and the others laughed, too.

In the center of the clump of bushes was a clear space, as smooth as the top of a table. In the middle of the smooth space grew a crooked tree with crooked branches. And, hanging from every branch were long reddish-brown things. Every once in a while one of the long reddish-brown things would wiggle itself loose from the branch and tumble down to the smooth place. Here it wiggled around and turned itself over and over while steam came from it. When the reddish-brown things sizzled and popped open, they slid across the smooth place and into a shallow dish of mustard where they turned over two or three times. They then hopped into a bun sliced through the center.

"Wild hot weenies!" Uncle Unk shouted as he reached over and caught up two of the weenies in the buns and started passing them to the others. Even Millicent ate two of the weenies before they had time to dip themselves in the mustard. Everyone felt very happy at such a pleasant ending to their sad visit to the Grotto of Greed.

As they sat around the weenie tree enjoying themselves to the full, Raggedy Ann thought she heard a tinkling back in the bushes and she went to see about it. There, within a stone's throw, she found a soda water spring bubbling from the ground. At the side of the spring was a syrup tree and at the end of each branch was a little sign marked, chocolate, strawberry, vanilla, and every flavor you could imagine. It was easy to fill a glass with as much flavor as one wanted, then hold it under the sizzling spray of the soda water spring to get a delicious, cold glass of soda water.

Perhaps the sodas would have been better if there had been some ice cream. But, since they could find no ice cream mud puddle nearby, everyone was contented.

After a while, when even Uncle Unk had eaten as many hot weenies as he wished, they all walked over beneath a big tree and sat down in the soft grass. Far across the valley the blue, blue of a great mountain raised its head towards the fleecy pop-corn clouds. And, there on top of the mountain stood the grand castle shining in the sunlight.

Everyone seemed to be growing very drowsy after eating so much at the weenie picnic. Uncle Unk had curled up on the grass with his head in Auntie Aunt's lap and was soon sound asleep. Millicent sat beside Raggedy Ann and went to sleep sitting up. But in a moment she opened her eyes and growled softly.

Chapter Six

A COW came walking out of the bushes and up to our friends. She was softly humming a tune and chewing her cud at the same time. It was a very satisfied, contented sound.

There was a friendly smile at the corners of the cow's mouth as she came up. "GLOOB," she said, swallowing, "Morning!" Then, with a chuckle, "I almost choked on the 'Good.' " She sat down and looked from one to another.

"Good morning!" Raggedy Ann laughed, "but it is really afternoon."

"Indeed, so it is," the cow agreed.

"We heard you singing softly as you came up," Auntie Aunt laughed.

"Hmm, my dear," the cow chuckled, "I was just sort of day-dreaming and humming to myself as I chewed my cud."

"You sounded very contented," Raggedy Andy remarked.

"Well, I certainly should," the cow said, "look at all the

great meadow covered with tender green grass. Could anyone wish for more? Indeed not!"

"I never knew that cows really and truly sang," Auntie Aunt said.

"Of course not," Uncle Unk said sleepily, "who said they did?"

"I did!" the cow replied.

"Have it your own way," Uncle Unk said and dropped off to sleep again.

"He's so tired," Auntie Aunt said with a note of apology in her voice.

"Yes," the cow said, and seemed about to say more when she changed her mind. Turning to Raggedy Ann, the cow asked, "Would you like to hear me sing the song I am composing for the County Fair?"

"I am sure we would all love it," Raggedy Ann replied.

The cow stretched her neck until her head was straight out from her body. "MOO-OOO," she started, then choked and coughed. Raggedy Ann patted her on the back while Raggedy Andy quickly brought a drink of cold water from the soda spring.

"I started to sing with my cud in my mouth, and no cow

cud do that, cud she?" and she laughed heartily at her joke.

"Cud you try again, Mrs. Cow?" Raggedy Andy laughed.

"I cud and I will," the cow replied, "because I am growing very fond of you folks."

The cow again stretched her neck and with a low "Moo, —just to get started on the right tones," she explained, the cow began singing in a soft low voice . . .

"Few persons give attention to the talents of a cow,
Somehow, somehow, the talents of a cow.
Forgive me if I mention in a chosen word or two,
A view, a view, of what a cow can do."

Uncle Unk sat up sleepily and started a little song of his own that went something like this . . .

"Oh, this is proving interesting.
I never knew a cow could sing."

The smile left the cow's face and she rolled her eyes in Uncle Unk's direction. "It isn't such a simple thing," the cow said, "so, please don't interrupt."

"It seems exasperating, the butting that we do,
Oh Moo, Oh Moo, the butting that we do
Is always turned to butter, when a butter way to do,
Is chew, is chew, upon a cud or two."

Raggedy Ann sang softly, in tune with the cow . . .

"But, you've forgotten, Mrs. Cow,
To sing your talents to us now."

"Lovely, my dear!" the cow said, "you have a sweet voice."

"I'm always thinking of my chow
Now, here's the chorus, it's a wow."

"Do you mean that you have a chorus to the song?" Millicent asked, glad that the song had not ended.

"Certainly, Millicent!" the cow replied, "the chorus is always the best part of the song. It's just like the grass in the next field."

"You mean the grass in the next field is better than the grass in this field?" Millicent asked.

"To be sure, Millicent!" the cow laughed, "every cow well-knows that. And, that is why every cow tries to get out of her own pasture into the one she thinks is greener."

"But, what if you are in the next pasture?" Millicent wanted to know.

"Then the grass is better in this pasture," the cow replied.

"I never heard anything quite so silly," Uncle Unk yawned drowsily.

"Nothing silly about that at all," the cow continued. "You just lack the cogitative ability to comprehend the mental activities which are flubbergating in the cranium of the gentle bovine."

The cow hesitated a moment so her friends could appreciate this last speech. Then she turned to Auntie Aunt and said, "I'll bet if I should ask Uncle Unk to explain why cows like to walk through flower beds, he wouldn't know what to

say. Nor could he tell you why we just dote on lying down in a nice bed of geraniums or nasturtiums."

"I am certain he does not know," Auntie Aunt laughed. "But won't you please sing the chorus of your song?"

"The discussion has made me forget the song I was singing."

"You were about to sing of the talents of a cow," Raggedy Ann reminded her.

"Oh yes! the talents of a cow. This is the chorus,—

Who is it grazes night and dawn,
And helps to manicure the lawn?
The cow! The cow! You're bright. Quite right,
Who, but the thoughtful cow?

Who is it gives the milk in turn,
To change to butter in the churn?
The cow! The cow! You're bright. Quite right.
It is the carefree cow.

Who gives the spareribs and beef steak,
The milk and butter for your cake?
Who gives dried beef and ice cream, too,
And hamburg steak, I ask of you?

The cowwww ow ow, The cowwww ow ow,
The modest, gentle cow."

They all applauded loudly when the cow had finished her song. "Very, very nice, Mrs. Cow," Raggedy Ann said.

"There are eight more verses, all as lovely as these. And when we cows get together at the County Fair and sing the whole song, it is going to be too lovely for words."

Millicent pricked up her toy puppydog ears, "Listen!" she said, "I hear a real-for-sure dog barking."

"Oh yes," the cow sighed, "it's Fido coming to drive me to the barn. It will soon be milking time, you know."

Fido came dashing up. "Trying to hide from me behind the bushes, were you?" he barked.

"Now don't nip my heels, Fido," Mrs. Cow said.

"Then you'd better hurry," Fido threatened.

"I shall go just as slowly as I wish, Mr. Fido," the cow told him.

"Oh, but they are mad at you up at the castle!" Fido cried. "You not only got into the garden and ate up all the lettuce and spinach, but you also slept in the Queen's prize flower bed last night. You'll catch it!"

"There!" the cow said, turning to her friends, "Isn't that just what I have been telling you? No one understands a cow."

"Come on, move along, Mrs. Cow," Fido barked. "Oh! you would try to kick me, would you?" said Fido nipping the heels of the cow and jumping quickly to one side.

The cow, with Fido at her heels, ran across the meadow as fast as she could go.

Raggedy Ann and the others laughed as they watched, for, the cow ran in just the opposite direction from the castle.

"Let's go home!" Auntie Aunt said, shaking Uncle Unk gently.

"I shall never go home," Uncle Unk said as he sat up and rubbed his eyes. "Why are we sitting here? Where is all my gold? Who hit me on the top of my head?"

"Now, now!" Auntie Aunt said soothingly, "Let us forget all that. You were rescued from the Grotto of Greed. Now we must return to our nice little store."

"Never!" Uncle Unk cried, "I remember the Golden Butterfly and I shall go to the castle and find it, now that you have taken my golden coins from me." And, before anyone could stop him, Uncle Unk jumped to his feet and went running across the meadow towards the mountain in the distance.

Auntie Aunt, Raggedy Ann, Raggedy Andy and little Millicent went trailing after him.

Uncle Unk led them a merry chase across the lovely meadow and into a forest, where, after a while, they came upon Uncle Unk all out of breath. He was sitting on a stone that had fallen from the walls of a tumble-down castle.

Vines covered the walls of the old ruin. Inside, where once were great rooms, large forest trees were growing.

"What a beautiful place it must have been years and years ago," Raggedy Andy sighed.

"Some of the walls are still standing," Raggedy Ann said. "Let us walk inside and see what there is to see."

Just as Raggedy Ann said this, a Golden Butterfly came fluttering over the tree tops. It circled the ruins three times and then flew inside to what had been the largest room.

"The Golden Butterfly! The Golden Butterfly!" Uncle

Unk cried excitedly as he scrambled over the fallen stones and disappeared within the walls of the castle.

The others followed through one room after another until they came to where Uncle Unk stood within a great room littered with fallen stones and timbers, which time had scattered upon the floor.

"There it is!" Uncle Unk cried, "The Golden Butterfly! Up on the ceiling!" He picked up a stone and was about to throw it at the butterfly when Raggedy Andy caught his arm.

"Do not throw at the butterfly, Uncle Unk!" Raggedy Andy said, "You might hit it and destroy it."

"I want it!" Uncle Unk cried, struggling to get free. "See how it shines in the darkness. Its wings are of gold."

And, true enough, the wings of the butterfly did, in the semidarkness, appear to be of gold. As the butterfly raised and lowered its wings, they shone with a soft golden light that cast a radiance upon the ceiling all around it. And as our friends watched, fascinated by the loveliness, the great room grew darker and the light from the Golden Butterfly increased. Then another butterfly came fluttering in and settled upon the ceiling beside the first one. As our friends

watched, other butterflies came pouring in until the ceiling was covered with the lovely creatures.

"See! what did I tell you?" Uncle Unk cried, "I knew that I would find them if I followed the first Golden Butterfly. Now I will catch all of them and . . ."

Auntie Aunt clapped her hand over Uncle Unk's mouth, and drew him back with the others into the shadow of a tall column. They could hear the toll of a distant bell. The sound seemed to come from high above them.

Seven times the bell tolled and then remained silent but the vibrations hummed on for a few moments. Then again the deep tones rolled through the ruins, five times and silence.

Our friends stood fascinated by the enchantment. The vibrations of the bell softened into silence. The Golden Butterfly raised and lowered her radiant wings and fluttered silently to the floor. The rest of the butterflies followed and grouped themselves behind the Golden Butterfly.

"Now I shall catch them!" Uncle Unk cried and would have dashed out into the room, but Raggedy Andy held him tightly. The great voice of the bell sounded again. Just once, it boomed.

Before the sound had faded entirely, the fallen stones and timbers of the ruined castle raised themselves silently in place. Pieces of broken furniture and torn draperies assembled and the great room was flooded with light. The Golden Butterfly raised and lowered her wings slowly, as steps sounded down the long hallway. A tall man dressed in the finest of silks and satins came walking into the great room. He approached the Golden Butterfly and tapped three times upon the marble floor with the long cane he carried. Then with the end, he touched the wing of the Golden Butterfly.

Instantly the form of the Golden Butterfly changed. And there stood the most radiant creature our friends had ever seen. She stood surrounded by ladies and gentlemen dressed in silks and satins.

"A Princess!" Raggedy Ann gasped.

The lovely Princess stood silently and proudly before the tall man. Again he rapped three times upon the floor with his cane. "Will you speak?" he cried in an angry voice.

The lovely eyes of the Princess seemed to glow with a light of hatred, but her voice was soft and flutelike. "I have nothing to say," she answered.

"You will not consent?" the man screamed, "even though I promise to lift the enchantment and restore all of the old time loveliness, just as you see it now?"

"Mang!" the Princess replied, "your power is great and

you have brought terrible misfortune upon us, but I shall never consent. You may work your evil enchantment and destroy the beauties of our castle, but your magic is not strong enough to overcome the love in my heart. Nor is it strong enough to overcome the love of those who are near and dear to me. Work your evil sorcery forever, if you will, but I will never agree. You will always remain just as far from attaining your evil desires."

"Fool, fool that you are!" Mang shouted. "Tomorrow night, I shall give you one more opportunity. Refuse me then, and I shall never again lift the enchantment from you and your people. This castle shall crumble to dust and I shall forget you."

"You shall never forget!" the Princess said. "Deep within your selfish heart a small voice will always remind you that you have destroyed all this loveliness. And that small voice will never let you know peace or happiness. Your heart will always be filled with remorse for the evils you have brought upon us. In true justice, as you know, you receive in exact measure as you give."

The face of the magician grew dark with anger. He struck the floor with his cane. Then, as his steps echoed down the long hallway, the lights disappeared and the ruins of the castle were in darkness.

Chapter Seven

HO HUM," Uncle Unk yawned, "I certainly had a good night's sleep."

Raggedy Ann rubbed her eyes and sat up. "I thought I was using Millicent for a pillow," she laughed. "I guess I must have rolled over in the night and Millicent has gone somewhere else to sleep."

"I did not close my eyes all night," Raggedy Andy said as he rose from the corner where he had been sitting.

"Wake up, Auntie Aunt!" Uncle Unk said as he shook Auntie Aunt gently. "We must get breakfast somewhere."

"Ah yes, breakfast," Auntie Aunt said sleepily, "where shall we find it?"

"I wonder where Millicent can be?" Raggedy Ann said as she and the others walked out of the ruined castle into the sunlight. She had hardly finished the question when Millicent came trotting up.

"I've just found the strangest thing you ever saw," Millicent said.

"We hope it is as strange as the wild hot weenies you found yesterday, Millicent," Raggedy Ann laughed.

"Come see!" Millicent said as she trotted to a little brook, jumped from one stepping stone to another and went into a clump of bushes. "There you are!" she said.

In a clearing there was a large flat stone and on the stone eight or ten pancakes were steaming. When they cooked to a golden brown, the pancakes flip-flopped from the large stone to small flat stones. The branch of a maple tree pointed itself at each pancake and, from the end of the branch, a stream of maple syrup flowed onto the hot pancake.

"Breakfast!" Uncle Unk exclaimed with joy.

Indeed, it was breakfast and everyone enjoyed it very much.

As our friends sat there enjoying the pancakes, the Golden Butterfly fluttered from one flower to another; and, although Uncle Unk watched it closely, he did not speak of it, nor did he attempt to catch it.

"I hope he has forgotten his silly idea about catching it," Raggedy Ann thought. "If he knew of the beautiful dream I had last night, he would never again want to capture the lovely creature."

When everyone had eaten as much breakfast as he wished, Uncle Unk strolled away down a little path through the forest. Auntie Aunt went with him and she was wondering why he had not mentioned the Golden Butterfly or said anything about his desire to get back the gold he had lost in the Grotto of Greed.

Raggedy Ann and Millicent walked over to where Raggedy Andy sat upon the bank of the brook. The three sat and watched the trout playing in the clear cool water and jumping for flies just above the surface.

"I had a wonderful dream last night," Raggedy Ann mentioned by way of starting a conversation. "It was so real and beautiful, but it ended so unhappily."

"Tell us about it," Raggedy Andy said.

"I dreamed we were all sitting in the shadows of the pillars of a great room in the ruins of the castle. The Golden Butterfly was there and fluttered down from the ceiling

when a great bell tolled."

"Did it toll seven times?" Millicent asked.

"Yes," Raggedy Ann replied with surprise, "seven times, then five, then once."

"And a tall man with a long cane came in and stood before a Princess?" Millicent again asked.

"How strange!" Raggedy Ann exclaimed. "Millicent must have had the same dream."

"My dears!" Raggedy Andy said, "I did not close my

J. GRUELLE

eyes all night. The rest of you went to sleep late in the night sometime. The dream, you mention, really happened. Even Uncle Unk saw it."

"That must be why he made no attempt to catch the Golden Butterfly this morning," Raggedy Ann said. "Uncle Unk knows the Golden Butterfly is really the lovely Princess who is under the spell of the evil Mang's enchantment."

"I wonder what will happen tonight when the enchant-

ment is lifted, as Mang promised, for the last time?" Raggedy Ann wondered out loud.

"I am sure the lovely Golden Butterfly Princess will again deny Mang's request, or, I should say, his demand," Raggedy Andy said.

Millicent touched Raggedy Ann upon the back very gently and then went trotting away down the path that Auntie Aunt and Uncle Unk had taken. When she had gone a few feet, Millicent turned and looked back at Raggedy Ann. Then she trotted on a few feet further and turned again, as if to say, "Come on Raggedy Ann I want to see you by yourself."

Raggedy Ann excused herself and left Raggedy Andy sitting beside the brook. She followed Millicent, who turned and saw Raggedy Ann coming but continued to trot on down the path.

Millicent stopped a little farther on at the fork of the path and waited until Raggedy Ann came up.

"What is it, Millicent?" Raggedy Ann asked.

"Last night, when Mang changed the beautiful Princess back into a butterfly and returned the castle to ruins, I followed him," Millicent whispered.

"Brave little Millicent!" Raggedy Ann said as she caught up the toy dog and hugged her. "Where did he go?"

"That is just where I am going to lead you now, Raggedy Ann," Millicent replied. "It was very dark and I got lost trying to get back to you before daybreak this morning, but, now I know the way. Please put me down so that I may follow my tracks by putting my nose to the ground."

Raggedy Ann thought this looked like the start of an adventure and she said to Millicent, "Let's go back and get Raggedy Andy. We may need his help."

"No, Raggedy Ann," and Millicent seemed positive, "I think it better for him to stay back and look after Auntie Aunt and Uncle Unk."

Millicent trotted along in front of Raggedy Ann until she came to a clearing in the forest. "Stop!" Millicent whispered, "As soon as Mang entered this clearing, he disappeared, so we had better not set foot in this cleared space. It is enchanted and I know it. Mang must have put a spell on the place so that if anyone at any time should follow him, he would know it at once. And he could capture or destroy whoever followed him."

"I am surely glad you did not follow him, Millicent," Raggedy Ann said.

"So am I, as you shall soon see," Millicent chuckled way down in her sawdust stuffing. Then she continued, "Just as

Mang started walking across this clearing last night, the moon came shining from behind a cloud, and I could see him plainly. As he walked he seemed to grow thin. . . ."

"Thin?" Raggedy Ann asked.

"Yes!" Millicent answered, "so thin, I could see right through him. And finally, he vanished completely."

"Then you tried to find your way back, and . . ."

"No!" Millicent said, "I ran around to the other side of the clearing and sat down behind a stone at the side of a little stream. Presently, I heard footsteps. And, do you know, Old Mang walked within twenty feet of me? He was terribly angry. I could hear him grit his teeth as he waved his arms and talked to himself."

"Could you hear what he said, Millicent?"

"Sometimes I heard," Millicent answered. "He said once, 'And, just to make certain that you shall never appear upon the scene again, I will put you where no living person will ever find you!' and he threw a bottle that he was holding in his hands."

"He threw a bottle, Millicent?" Raggedy Ann asked.

"A tiny bottle," Millicent replied. "Mang threw the bottle into the brook at a spot where it roars and tumbles into a tunnel in the side of the hill. 'There!' he cried as he shook his fist, 'you start your journey into the earth and no one shall ever bring you to light again!' " Millicent chuckled softly to herself as she added, "And what a silly thing Mang is with all his magic knowledge."

"What in the world do you mean, Millicent?" Raggedy Ann asked.

"I will show you, right now, just what I mean, Raggedy Ann," Millicent laughed. "For, as soon as Mang turned and went back into the clearing, I jumped into the brook and went tumbling head over heels through the roar and foam of the water into the darkness where the brook disappeared into the tunnel in the side of the hill."

"Why, Millicent!" Raggedy Ann exclaimed.

"And," Millicent laughed, "I am taking you right to the place where the brook comes out of the other side of the hill. That silly Mang has probably never bothered to look that far. Isn't he stupid?"

Millicent trotted along for more than an hour with Raggedy Ann close behind. They came at last to where the brook flowed deep and silently out of the hill and beneath the giant trees of the forest. They followed along the bank for a short distance where they came upon a sand bar. Millicent stopped and said, "Here is the spot where I came out of the water and I will show you what Mang threw into the roaring brook where it enters the other side of this hill." Millicent led the way out upon the sand bar and began scratching in the sand. Soon she uncovered a tiny little bottle which looked as though it was made of blue glass. There were strange mystical characters in white and the top of the bottle had been sealed with a very hard substance that was melted on.

"Isn't it strange?" Raggedy Ann remarked as she picked up the bottle and turned it over and over in her hands. "I wonder what is inside of it?"

"Whatever it may be, we are sure it is something Mang hated very much; so, it must be something very good," Millicent said.

"Let us get back to Auntie Aunt and Uncle Unk and Raggedy Andy," Raggedy Ann suggested. "We must get their advice."

Chapter Eight

"HE'S gone!" Raggedy Ann exclaimed when she and Millicent came to the bank of the brook where they had left Raggedy Andy.

Millicent put her nose to the ground and circled around. "He started to follow us, I guess," she said.

"Can you tell by smelling the ground whether Auntie Aunt and Uncle Unk returned here?" Raggedy Ann asked.

"They did not return," Millicent replied. "Perhaps Raggedy Andy grew uneasy at Auntie Aunt and Uncle Unk staying away so long, and has started out to hunt them."

"I am sorry we were away such a long time," Raggedy Ann said.

"I thought it best that just you go with me to get the bottle," Millicent said. "I was afraid that with Raggedy Andy with us, Mang might discover us."

"You were quite right, Millicent," Raggedy Ann agreed.

"You haven't had anything to eat since breakfast," Millicent said to Raggedy Ann. "Suppose you have some of the

pancakes and maple syrup while I run and see if I can find our friends before it gets dark."

"I think I should go with you, Millicent," Raggedy Ann said.

"Now, I can run very fast and I do not tire easily," Millicent laughed, "so, you go on over to the pancake place and I will be back in a short time."

Without waiting for a reply, Millicent went running down the path. And Raggedy Ann walked over to where the pancakes were sizzling on the flat stone.

It was long after sundown and darkness was settling over the forest when Millicent returned.

"You did not find them?" Raggedy Ann asked in alarm.

"No," Millicent replied, "I followed their tracks as far as the clearing where Mang lives. I know Raggedy Andy walked right into it. I was afraid to follow farther. Not on my own account," Millicent hastened to explain, "but because I did not want to have anything happen to me that would cause you to be left here all alone."

"Thank you, Millicent!" Raggedy Ann said as she hugged the toy dog close to her heart.

"Have you the bottle?" Millicent asked.

"Here in my pocket," Raggedy Ann replied patting her apron pocket.

"Could you find any trace of Auntie Aunt and Uncle Unk?" Raggedy Ann asked Millicent.

"Yes, I could tell their tracks were underneath those of Raggedy Andy," Millicent replied, "and that they had walked into the enchanted clearing early in the day."

"Dear me!" was all Raggedy Ann could say.

"Shall we leave the ruins of the castle and return across the meadow?" Millicent wished to know. "I can easily find the way, even in the dark."

"No, let us stay here," Raggedy Ann decided.

"You are not afraid?" Millicent asked.

"Not at all," Raggedy Ann said with assurance. "Let us go into the great hall where we saw the Golden Butterfly Princess last night."

Chapter Nine

THE Golden Butterfly fluttered down from the tree tops and flew slowly along above the ground. The light from its radiant wings threw a soft glow on the fallen stones and timbers, so that Raggedy Ann could quite easily find her way into the great hall of the ruined castle.

Raggedy Ann and Millicent hid behind the tall columns and watched. The Golden Butterfly again flew in and alighted on the ceiling. She was promptly followed by her many followers, just as the night before.

The great voice of the bell boomed . . . seven times . . . then five . . . then one.

Footsteps were heard coming up the long hallway and the Magician, with Auntie Aunt, Uncle Unk and Raggedy Andy before him, came in.

Mang struck the floor three times with his cane. Instantly the old castle returned to its splendor and the butterflies changed to the beautiful Princess and her court.

"Will you speak?!!" Mang shouted.

And again the Princess replied quietly, "I have nothing to say."

"Who are these persons I find wandering through my enchanted clearing?" Mang asked the Princess.

"They are strangers to me," the Princess replied.

"They are friends of yours!" Mang yelled. "I knew it the moment they entered my enchanted clearing."

"Then, if they are friends of mine," the Princess replied, "it is because they know of my unfortunate enchantment,

and not because I know them."

"What the Princess says is true," Raggedy Andy said. "We were here last night and watched you."

"So!" Mang shrieked, shaking his fist under Raggedy Andy's nose, "you came here spying, did you? Well, I will attend to you later."

Then turning to the Princess, the Magician asked, "Do you consent? Answer at once, for this is the last time I shall release the enchantment over you and your people and your castle."

"I have not changed my mind in the slightest since last night. I shall never consent!" the Princess replied.

"Then, before I leave, let me tell you that I have destroyed Prince Adrian. You may as well give your consent for you will never see him again."

The Princess drew herself up proudly and folded her arms across her breast, but remained silent.

"Once more, and only once, I give you the opportunity of saving yourself and your people!" Mang shouted.

The Princess remained silent.

Mang waited a moment, as though considering everything in his mind, and then said in a terrible voice, "I have given you your last chance." He raised his cane as if to strike the Princess. . . . Raggedy Andy's arm shot out, catching the Magician squarely on the chin. As Raggedy Andy leaped to strike again, the Magician brought his heavy cane down on Raggedy Andy's head and knocked him to the floor.

Uncle Unk sprang into the fray at this point but was promptly laid out with a well directed blow from Mang's cane. At this, Auntie Aunt began screaming, which added greatly to the excitement.

Millicent, puppydog, wiggled out of Raggedy Ann's arms and dashed wildly at Mang. She snapped her rag jaws about his leg and held on. The hateful Magician reached down and pulled the rag dog away. Then Raggedy Ann, who had been standing spellbound watching the excitement, rushed from hiding just as Mang with strong hands tore Millicent to pieces and threw her to the floor.

Raggedy Ann cried out in frenzy at this, and taking the bottle from her pocket, she threw it with all her strength at Mang. The Magician turned at Raggedy Ann's sharp cry just enough so that the bottle struck him fairly upon his temple. With a sigh, he crumpled to the floor.

The bottle bounced from Mang's temple and fell with a crash to the marble floor.

As the bottle broke, a cloud of smoke arose from the spot. There, in the cloud, was a handsome young man. He took in the situation at a glance and, drawing his sword, he placed its point at the throat of the prostrate Magician.

Raggedy Ann ran up to the fallen Magician and tore his purse from its golden chain. "Here are Mang's magical charms," she cried as guards stepped out from among the

Princess' courtiers and bound the Magician hand and foot, "and I will try to use them right away to bring brave little Millicent back to life."

Raggedy Ann's eyes filled with tears so that she could scarcely see what she was doing. But, she gathered the pieces of the little, toy puppydog into a neat pile. Around this she drew a mystic circle with a piece of chalk taken from Mang's purse.

J. GRUELLE

Raggedy Ann took the magic charms from the purse. She waved them above the torn pieces of cloth and the little pile of sawdust, as she went round and round the pile singing,—

"Magic, Magic, work for me,
Do not let misfortune be
The reward for bravery.
Magic, Magic, tell me whether
Millicent will come together."

Everyone gave a glad cry. They saw the torn pieces of brave, little Millicent gather. Each in its proper place. With a shake of her little rag body and with her funny little stubby tail wagging happily, Millicent ran from the mystic circle and, with joyful barks, jumped into Raggedy Ann's arms.

"It didn't hurt even a teeny-weeny speck," Millicent laughed.

The lovely Golden Butterfly Princess with her arm about Prince Adrian had the court physician bandage Raggedy Andy's head and the bump on Uncle Unk's head, while the castle guards carried the magician, Mang, off to prison for safe keeping.

Prince Adrian led the lovely Princess to the throne and asked Raggedy Ann, Auntie Aunt, Raggedy Andy and Uncle Unk to take seats right near them. Millicent went along in Raggedy Ann's arms.

The ladies and gentlemen of the court gathered in front of the Prince and Princess. The hearts of all were filled with rejoicing and happiness now that the horrid spell was broken. From behind a bank of flowers at the side of the throne, an orchestra was playing softly.

"Raggedy Ann," the Princess said as she motioned Raggedy Ann to her and gave her a big kiss, "Prince Adrian and I owe our present happiness to you and your nice friends. We want to reward you for breaking the spell of the wicked Mang. Ask whatever you desire. If it is within our power, your wish shall be granted."

"Oh, thank you, Golden Butterfly Princess!" Raggedy Ann exclaimed joyfully, "but, little toy puppydog, Millicent, is the real one to be rewarded. It was Millicent who followed Mang when he left here last night. Millicent saw Mang throw the bottle into the underground brook. It was she who jumped into the dark waters of the roaring brook and followed the bottle through the tunnel in the hill, finally recovering it and burying it safely in the sand bar. Then, when Millicent led me to the spot and dug up the bottle, I put it in my pocket. So, you see, brave little Millicent should really have the reward. For me, the friendship of you and the Prince and your good people, is enough reward."

"Raggedy Ann!" the Princess said as she put her arm around the dear old doll and drew her closer, "You are a dear. I will reward Millicent, and at once." And, stooping over, the Princess caught up Millicent and hugged the toy dog to her heart. When she returned Millicent to Raggedy Ann's arms, everyone noticed that the puppydog wore a golden collar with a jewelled bell as a pendant.

The Princess then wished to reward Auntie Aunt, Uncle Unk and Raggedy Andy, but each declined just as Raggedy Ann had done.

"Tomorrow we shall have a grand celebration and in the evening a wonderful ball in which we will all join," the Princess proclaimed. "Let us get a good night of rest."

Chapter Ten

THE next day, the beautiful castle was the scene of great activity in preparation for the grand ball.

The Princess sent for Raggedy Ann and her friends to come to the throne room just after luncheon.

The lovely Princess and Prince Adrian were awaiting our friends and asked them to be seated close by on the throne dais.

"I have sent for you to ask your advice about Mang," the Princess began when all were comfortably seated. "But first let me tell you something of our unfortunate enchantment."

"Years ago," the Princess continued, "before Prince Adrian and I were married, Mang was the prime minister of the kingdom next to mine. You may have seen the great castle upon the distant mountain top."

"Ah, yes!" Uncle Unk sighed, "I thought the Golden Butterfly lived at that great castle."

"No," the Princess smiled, "I have always lived here.

Mang used to visit us often and always brought wonderful presents from the King of the Rainbow Towers. We called the castle by that name, for, after every storm we always saw a rainbow stretching over the beautiful castle."

"Then," she continued, "Prince Adrian came from the country to the south and we were happily married. A short time after this, Mang visited us. He wanted me to give up Prince Adrian and return with him to the Rainbow Towers. He told me he had enchanted the King and Queen of Rainbow Towers and had set himself up as King."

"Of course, I would never consent to such a terrible scheme, for I loved Prince Adrian. When I told Mang what a selfish, wicked, creature I thought he was, he flew into a rage. Prince Adrian came in just at that moment, and Mang, taking out his magic charms, cast a spell over the Prince and put him in the bottle. The cruel Mang told me Prince Adrian would remain in the bottle forever, unless I consented to his wicked plan. I told Mang I would never agree."

The Princess continued. "Every night for five nights, Mang came to me just as the great bell tolled seven times, then five times, then only once. And each time he threatened me with great misfortune if I would not consent. On the

fifth night, when I again refused him, Mang became so angry, he cast his horrible enchantment over all of us. I became a Golden Butterfly. My ladies and gentlemen of the court were changed to golden butterflies. The castle tumbled in ruins about us."

"What a dreadful thing to do," Uncle Unk cried, "I'd like to tweek his long nose."

"And get another blow upon your head with the cane," Auntie Aunt laughed as she hugged Uncle Unk.

"Night before last," the Princess continued, "I flew into the ruins of the throne room as you know, for you were here and saw and heard everything. Last night when Raggedy Ann threw the bottle and released the Prince, Mang was taken off his guard. Now, Raggedy Ann has Mang's magical charms, and with these she can perform great feats of magic. I have asked you to come here to advise us what to do with Mang. While he was heartless in his cruelty to us, Prince Adrian and I have no desire for revenge in our hearts."

No one spoke for several minutes after the Princess finished, finally, Prince Adrian said, "Raggedy Ann, please give us your thoughts."

"Mang, the magician, was truly wicked and selfish in his desires," Raggedy Ann began. "For that reason he should be punished. Those of us who are kind, should never let the tenderness of our hearts affect our good judgment. Often a person who has done a great wrong, is pardoned by those in authority who feel sorry. Soon after the wrongdoer is pardoned, he commits a far worse wrong than the one before. So, we should try to avoid this."

"What you say is surely true," the Princess agreed.

"Suppose you send for Mang?" Raggedy Ann suggested, "and let me talk with him."

When Mang was brought before them, still in chains, the Princess said, "Mang, we have brought you here to pass judgment and punish you for the wrongs you have done. Have you anything to say?"

"Yes!" Mang answered boldly, "if I had to do it all over again, I would do the same. I wanted power and the thrill of ruling the Kingdom of the Rainbow Towers. I schemed and worked until that power was mine. Then," turning to the Princess, he continued, "I wanted you. And I shall never outgrow that desire."

"Dear me!" Auntie Aunt cried, "The wicked creature is making it harder for himself all the time."

"Mang!" Raggedy Ann said in a soft voice, "how would you like to be shut up in a tiny bottle for years and be thrown into an underground river, never to see the light of day again?"

"Not that!" the Magician cried, falling upon his knees before Raggedy Ann. "That would be too terrible. Not that. Please do not put me in a bottle. Do anything else you wish, but please do not do that."

"You did that to Prince Adrian," Raggedy Ann said, her shoe button eyes flashing. She took Mang's purse from her pocket and held the magical charms in the palm of her hand. Mang rolled upon the floor at her feet and whined in his terror.

"Before I work the magic of your own charms upon you, you wicked creature," Raggedy Ann said. "I shall find out what you did to the King and Queen of the Rainbow Towers. For, they may still be under your wicked enchantment."

Raggedy Ann drew a circle around the kneeling form of the Magician. She waved the charms above his head and cried, "Through the magic of these charms, I command you

to tell me exactly what you did to the king and queen."

Mang tried not to reply, but the magic could not be overcome. "I changed them into an old man and old woman and sent them away out of the country."

"Where did you send them, you selfish man?" Raggedy Ann asked.

"I do not know the name of the place," Mang replied. "I just made the magic wish that they would disappear into another country, and they disappeared."

"Then I shall work the magic charms to bring them here before us," Raggedy Ann cried, "and you will have them to answer to as well as to the Prince and Princess."

Raggedy Ann held the charms in her hand and made the wish that the King and Queen of the Rainbow Towers should stand before her. Nothing happened for several moments and the Magician broke the silence with a hard cruel laugh. "Aha!" he cried, "the charms do not work for you."

"The charms have worked," Raggedy Ann replied. "Isn't it a strange thing, Mang, your downfall was brought about directly by the King and Queen, whom you had enchanted?" Raggedy Ann pointed to Auntie Aunt and Uncle Unk and said, "The magic charms could not bring them from the far country since they were already here."

"You mean that we are the King and Queen of the Rainbow Towers, Raggedy Ann?" Auntie Aunt asked in astonishment.

"Indeed, that is true!" Raggedy Ann replied. "Uncle Unk wished to go to the castle of the Rainbow Towers when he was chasing the Golden Butterfly, and now he shall have his wish."

"Hold on, Raggedy Ann!" Uncle Unk cried as he ran up to her and caught her hand. "I do not wish to go there now. I do not wish to be rich. I do not wish to be a king. I just want to remain plain Uncle Unk and have Auntie Aunt with me at our nice little store. I want to go home now. Please let us all go back to our little store."

"Just the same," Raggedy Ann said, "I shall change you back into the persons you were when you were King and Queen. Then, if you wish to return to the little store,

you may do so." And, Raggedy Ann waved the magical charms above the heads of Auntie Aunt and Uncle Unk and they changed immediately into a young lady and a young man, not much older in appearance than the Prince and Princess.

"Ha!" Uncle Unk cried, when he saw the Magician kneeling before him, "What are you doing here, you wicked creature?" Then Uncle Unk remembered and laughed, "I was so surprised at the change in my appearance, I forgot for the moment that I was not Uncle Unk."

"You are the King of the Rainbow Towers," Mang said, "and the Queen is standing beside you."

"I shall not be a king," Uncle Unk cried, "I will not have it."

"And I prefer to be just plain Auntie Aunt," the Queen said.

"Why not let us all go to the kingdom of the Rainbow Towers and have a grand party for Raggedy Ann and Raggedy Andy and make them king and queen?" Auntie Aunt, now changed back to the Queen, suggested.

"You must all stay right here for the great celebration this evening," the Princess said. "My goodness! you are all so firm in not wishing to be kings or queens, you make

me want to return with you to your little store and not be a Princess." And she laughed merrily.

"We would love to have you," Auntie Aunt said.

"Now, what about Mang?" the Princess asked. "His enchantment of the king and queen did not turn out so badly for them, if they prefer the little store to their kingdom."

"I have thought of a plan," Raggedy Ann told the Princess. "With your permission I shall, with the magic charms, make Mang forget all of his former selfish schemes. I will hang a very tiny bottle by a chain about his neck. A bottle which he can never lose. And, listen well, Mang," Raggedy Ann cautioned, "Under the magic spell, if you ever so much as think an unkind, selfish or dishonest thought, you will find yourself shut up within the tiny golden bottle and the bottle will vanish forever."

"Thank you! Thank you!" Mang cried, "I shall make amends for all of my former misdeeds, Raggedy Ann."

When Mang had gone, Raggedy Ann handed the magic charms to the Golden Butterfly Princess saying, "I want you to have these, for, I know the magic you work will always be for good."

"Indeed it will!" the Princess promised as she kissed and hugged Raggedy Ann.

Just then there was a blast from the herald's trumpets. It was time to get ready for the ball. They all went to their rooms to dress for the big event. And, you may be sure the great ball was one of the loveliest ever seen this side of Fairyland.

The Golden Butterfly Princess and Prince Adrian had grown so fond of Raggedy Ann and her friends, they wanted them all to stay and live right there at the castle. But Raggedy Ann and Raggedy Andy were anxious to get back home and Uncle Unk and Auntie Aunt and Millicent were just as eager to return to their pleasant little magic store.

The Princess had the royal coach drawn by six white horses, brought around and Uncle Unk, Auntie Aunt and Millicent after many goodbyes, rode home to find the lovely little store just as they had left it.

The Princess then ordered her private aeroplane. For the first time, Raggedy Ann and Raggedy Andy found themselves being strapped into parachutes.

With many sincere goodbyes and promises to return, the Raggedys were off.

It seemed but a minute or two when the pilot turned to them and cried, "JUMP!"

Raggedy Ann went out one side and Raggedy Andy out the other. And, would you believe it? Raggedy Ann landed right on the porch roof outside the nursery window and Raggedy Andy found himself just in front of the playhouse.

The sun was just peeping over the horizon as the Raggedys scampered back to their places of the night before and not one of the real-for-sure people had any idea of the wonderful adventure.